GW01458549

GARY GIBSON

Scienceville & Other Lost Worlds

First edition

This book was professionally typeset on Reedsy.
Find out more at reedsy.com

Contents

Foreword

This is a collection of two novelettes and three short stories.

I don't write a great deal of short fiction for the usual reason: books pay a lot better, and tend to get a lot more attention. Also, short stories are hard - harder, in truth, than novels. Every now and then, though, some notion or idea persists until it's finally set down.

The other, really hard part about short stories is actually making them short. The first draft of *Scienceville* ran to thirteen thousand words. Getting it down to just eight thousand was a battle. These days, the optimum length, really, is about two thousand words. Fiction is increasingly published online, and two thousand words pretty much hits the sweet spot so far as the human attention span goes. My first ever published short story, *Mother Love*, in *Skeleton Crew* magazine way back in the very early 90s, was just under two thousand words. I haven't managed to write anything that short since.

This isn't a comprehensive collection, by any means. There are several stories I could have included, including *Mother Love*. I didn't, because they're from early in my career and I like to think I'm a better writer now than I was then. Those early stories were published at occasional intervals throughout the 1990s.

With the exception of *The Ranch*, which dates from the early 2000s, all of these stories were written after 2014. Scienceville first appeared in *Interzone*, *Senseless* in *Shoreline of Infinity* and *The Ranch* in an anthology called *Thirty Years of Rain*.

Two stories - *Guatemala* and *The Long Fall* - are previously unpublished. *The Long Fall* is set in the same universe as *Extinction Game* and *Survival Game*, my most recent books published by Tor, and features many of the same characters.

Scienceville

'Congratulations,' said Chase, when Joel showed him the letter. 'Looks like you've got your first stalker.'

'Let me see.' Phil yanked the letter out of Chase's hand. 'And she says she lives in Scienceville?' He darted a look at Joel. 'Oh man. Even *I* don't get ones that crazy.'

'Asshole.' Joel snatched the letter back. 'She doesn't say she lives there.'

A look passed between the two other men. 'No, just that she used to,' said Chase.

'Which isn't at all weird,' said Phil, 'what with Scienceville not actually existing and all.'

Over on the far side of the teacher's lounge Janice Glynn, who taught art, gave them a leery eye from above a chipped mug reading World's Best Cat Mom.

Joel's face reddened.

'Ignore Miss Havisham,' said Phil, dropping his voice. 'Please tell me you're not actually going to write back to her.'

Joel forced a laugh. 'Not a chance. She's obviously crazy. Anyone who'd write a letter like that has to be.'

'Assuming it's really a she,' said Chase.

Phil snapped his fingers. 'Might be a he. A truck driver. Some sweaty forty-stone guy who lives in a basement.' He rubbed his chin as if in thought. 'Who else do we know spends most of his time in a basement?'

'Hey, screw you,' said Joel. 'I didn't need to show either of you the damn letter.'

Phil put his hands up. 'Okay. No offence intended. Maybe this isn't the best place to talk about it,' he added, glancing towards Janice.

'You'd better just hope she never hears what you call her,' muttered Chase.

The end of recess came, and Joel spent the rest of that afternoon teaching. He wondered if he should have told Phil and Chase about the photograph that came with the letter, or that it wasn't even the first such letter he'd received.

* * *

A month before, a film crew from KSTV had interviewed Joel and some of the other artists taking part in the Fountain Grove Gallery's annual 'outsider art' exhibition. They'd given Joel just enough space for a couple of boroughs, and nothing more. He'd stood before a blown-up poster of one of Scienceville's main districts while a reporter with carefully blow-dried hair asked why he'd spent a significant fraction of his adult life designing enormous, intricately detailed maps of a place that didn't exist.

Scienceville, Joel explained to the increasingly bemused reporter, was a utopian community he'd dreamed up as a kid. It was a place where advanced scientific research for the genuine betterment of mankind could be carried out free of interference. Then he spent the rest of the evening watching people hurry by his exhibit on their way to see Gwen Frith's fine-art renditions of scenes from hardcore porn films with monkeys replacing the actors.

The next morning, he caught his interview on KSTV's

morning show. He'd been cut down to a ten-second soundbite that made him look deranged.

The first letter arrived shortly afterward, care of the gallery, all the way from France. It had been written on a manual typewriter by some guy called Fredrick Milan who insisted not only that Scienceville was real, but that he'd been dreaming about it and painting pictures of it since he was young. He was old, which went some way to explaining the avoidance of email.

Joel googled Milan and found pictures of an old, crumpled-looking man with a crooked nose and eyes that gleamed from beneath a hairless scalp. More, he was a real artist - and a renowned one, at that.

Joel kept browsing until he found some of Milan's work, but there was nothing even vaguely reminiscent of Scienceville. Most of Milan's paintings consisted of swirling abstracts, or near-blank canvases with tiny smears in one corner - all of which sold for a lot of money.

Milan wanted Joel to get in touch at the soonest opportunity, but Joel just shoved the letter inside one of many folders of sketches shelved in the basement where he worked on Scienceville. More than likely, the old man's mental faculties were declining with age.

By contrast, the second letter - also sent care of the gallery - made him wonder if he was the one losing his grip on reality.

I read about you online, the letter read. *I grew up in Scienceville, and even though it was a very long time ago and I was very small, I do remember that Newton Avenue isn't parallel to Atomic Road. Instead, they cross over each other - and the Halls of Justice are east of Bohr Parks, not west.*

It was from a woman called Natalie Donaldson, in Scotland. She explained she'd asked the gallery for his email, but they refused. Clearly, the gallery owners had no similar qualms about forwarding snail-mail.

There were more details than just that. At first, when he saw she'd accurately named places on the map, Joel got a shiver down his spine. But then he remembered the gallery had scanned portions of Scienceville and put them online, most particularly the section where Newton Avenue and Atomic Road were shown running north and south through Bohr Parks. She must, he realised, have gotten the details from there.

She, too, wanted him to write back, although she was vague as to why. It occurred to Joel the letter might actually be from Milan, or from someone else entirely, pretending to be both people. It simply wasn't possible that two strangers could independently write to him acting like a place he'd invented as a kid was real. So when he got home Thursday evening, he shoved Natalie Donaldson's letter into the same place he'd put Milan's, so he didn't have to think any more about either of them.

* * *

That evening, like every other since Dale and his mother passed, stretched out like a long and empty highway. He ate and watched TV, then made his way down to the basement, switching on the overhead lights before stepping up close to the outer edge of Waverley Borough, one of the newer outlying districts.

Over the last five years Scienceville had spread, sheet by sheet and district by district, until it covered very nearly the entire basement floor, except for a narrow margin around the edges. Detailed drawings and sketches of its principal architecture were pinned on the walls all around. The city was a smorgasbord of influences drawn from Buckminster Fuller, Le Corbusier, Frank Lloyd Wright, Ebenezer Howard, Fritz Lang's Metropolis, and Korda's vision of Everytown. Dozens and dozens of sheets of paper of varying sizes were carefully arranged according to a key system scrawled on the back of each, indicating how that sheet linked to each of its neighbours.

The whole thing was laid on a series of rubber mats that were a lot easier on the knees than the basement's concrete floor. A small plastic crate sat next to the boiler where he kept pencils, erasers, tape, crayons and paints. For some reason he'd never been able to envision what lay beyond Scienceville's borders: it was as if the town was its own self-contained universe, part of yet separate from the wider world.

One wall of the basement was almost entirely hidden behind a row of tall Ikea bookshelves he'd scored off Craigslist, their shelves crammed with file boxes where he kept the rest of the city: Scienceville was now much too big to fit on the floor in its entirety, so much of it was stored according to a catalogue system he'd invented. There were also a number of books on city planning and architecture, some well-thumbed and some hardly touched, and nearly a dozen volumes of history. Yet more boxes contained detailed histories of Scienceville's origins, and major events that had occurred since its founding.

Waverley was shaping up to be a new district on the absolute periphery of Scienceville. Most of the high street was still missing; Joel didn't need to refer to any of his files to know that following the Nuclear Treaty of 1962, negotiated and signed in Scienceville's Halls of Justice, there had been an influx of East Germans and Russians once nuclear weapons facilities on both sides of the Iron Curtain began to shut down. Most of the new immigrants, Joel had decided, would have wound up in

Waverley, and would almost certainly have arrived with pretty specific requirements when it came to their culinary habits. Waverley's high street shops would need to sell both Russian and German food, and books and newspapers in both languages as well.

Joel sat by the desk, opened his Macbook and spent the next hour browsing for books on German and Russian immigration, until he found what he needed and clicked *Buy*.

* * *

'So,' said Chase on Friday morning, 'my cousin's back in town. Sherylyn? Who just got divorced?'

Phil let out a soft groan from across the teacher's lounge, his laptop balanced on his knees. Chase glared at him, but Phil just grinned around the bagel half-wedged into his mouth.

'You met Sherylyn, right?' asked Chase, turning back to Joel.

'Didn't she get married just last year…?'

Chase made a face. 'Didn't last long. Just moved back here for a job. Maybe you could…take her out and show her around?'

Max grunted around his bagel. 'You don't want her, *I'll* take her.'

'Shut up, Phil. You're a pig.' Chase looked hard at Joel. 'You'd be doing me a favour. Otherwise she's going to sit around all evening at home with Marge bitching about her ex and I'll have to listen.'

'I'd love to,' said Joel. Chase's face brightened. 'But maybe some other time.'

'Don't be so pushy,' said Phil, putting his laptop back in his duffel bag and moving towards the door. 'But if he's not available, I am.'

'*You* have a reputation,' said Chase. 'And not a good one.

6

Joel…'

Joel stood. 'I'll think about it.'

'You mean no,' said Chase. 'You always mean no.'

'I'll see you Saturday.'

'How long's it been, Joel? Getting on what, four years?'

'Five,' said Joel, stepping towards the door Phil was holding open. 'Let Phil take her. He knows more places.'

Phil nodded vigorously. 'I know all the best restaurants.'

'You know,' Chase said to Phil, 'there's a reason Marge made me promise not to tell you she was back in town. Joel, I-'

Joel just shook his head, laughing, and let the door swing shut behind him.

'Saturday at six!' Chase yelled through the closed door. 'Barnaby's before the game!'

* * *

The next day, Joel arrived at Barnaby's to find Sherylyn sitting alone in a booth.

She darted a look at him. 'You're not-' She closed her eyes. 'Ah, Jesus.'

Joel looked down at her, then at the other, mostly empty booths reaching into the dim interior of the bar. He couldn't see Chase, or anybody else he knew.

'Sherylyn,' he said, sitting across from her. 'I guess we've been set up.'

She peered at him. 'Did you know…?'

'Not a clue.' She fixed him with a look and he raised his hands. 'Hands up. It's the truth.'

She pushed at a paper napkin, then sat back, shaking her head. 'Marge…I'm gonna kill that fucking girl. I told her not to…' She glanced at him through a tuft of hair. 'Look, it's not that you're not-'

'It's fine.' Joel shrugged. 'We could call it a night and engage in some angry texting, or…'

She looked at the door, then at Joel, then towards the bar, tapping long fingernails on the table top.

'What the hell,' she said at last. 'You couldn't possibly be worse than the last guy she set me up with.'

'How did that go?'

'We got married. You going to buy me a drink or not?'

* * *

They talked small stuff for the next couple hours, how little San Jose had changed since they'd both graduated, Sherylyn a few years after Joel. She'd gone to work in the New York Museum Archives before getting married and nearly as quickly divorced.

She gradually moved around the booth until they were sitting side by side and touched his arm a couple of times. She'd known Dale, but only from a distance, Dale having graduated when Sherylyn was still finishing high school.

'Marge mentioned you were known as an artist these days.'

He took a sip of his Moosehead. 'You really want to know?'

She nodded, and he told her about Scienceville, and how it brought focus back into his life after Dale died. To his surprise, she didn't get the judgemental look people sometimes did.

In fact, it wasn't long before she asked if she could see it.

* * *

She knelt on the floor by his side, peering down at the streets and alleys and buildings laid out across the basement floor, then up at the myriad sketches Joel had pinned to the walls to help him construct the map in all its myriad, swirling colours.

8

'This is amazing, Joel,' she said. 'I had no idea it was so…so detailed. And you really just made all of this up?'

'I…sure.' He nodded.

She laughed, her shoulder brushing his. By the time they'd found a taxi, they were both so drunk they were having to hold each other upright. 'You don't sound sure.'

'After all this time, it feels real to me.'

'What about the rest of the world?' she asked. 'Is it like Scienceville…wherever Scienceville is?'

'Honestly, I don't know. I never really thought about it for some reason.'

She put her hand over his, her gaze only slightly unfocused. 'So what made you start it?'

'The world's full of failed utopias, some good, some bad, some crazy. I just wanted to imagine one that worked.' He winced. 'I was only thirteen when I thought it up, and I didn't have any idea how things really worked.' He'd used the coloured pens that came with the Vintage Craft Master World of Plants Poster Set his father gave him just a week before he walked out on Joel and his mother. 'I put it away soon enough, but all those years later, after…' He shrugged.

She gave him a sympathetic look. 'I heard all about the accident.'

'Mom was driving, Dale was beside her. Ice on the road, the truck driver lost control…' he shrugged and forced a smile. 'I guess that makes all this a coping mechanism.'

She was silent a moment, then leaned in to kiss him. Her lips, thought Joel, tasted of jasmine and cherries.

'Well, Marge did say you were a bit different,' she said when she pulled back. 'Maybe you could show me the rest of your place?'

* * *

He woke in the morning alone and half-wrapped in his bed-sheets to find a text message on his phone. *Thanks Joel. It's been a lousy week and a lousy year and you did a lot to make me feel better about myself. Take care - Sherylyn.*

Something in the words told him he wouldn't be seeing her again. For the first time in a long while he found himself wondering where he'd be in another five years, and if he'd still be on his own.

After breakfast, he made his way back down to the basement, intent on clearing up, and found he'd opened the folder where he'd put the two letters. He picked up the second one, from Natalie Donaldson, and read it again.

What the hell, he thought: you only live once.

* * *

Dear Ms Donaldson,
Thanks for your letter. I'm going to have to disagree with you about Atomic Road and Newton Avenue because I remember them incredibly well. Matter of fact, my parents worked at the particle research lab right where they intersect (the same lab, by the way, run by Dr Wu, after he escaped a Chinese prison through the fifth dimension). Were you there when the giant radioactive gorilla tried to climb up the top of the Halls of Justice back in 1998?
Anyway, thanks for sharing your thoughts.
- Joel Kincaird.

He couldn't help smirking to himself right after he posted the letter. *Giant radioactive gorilla. Let's see how she likes that.*

The reply came back just ten days later:

> Hi Joel,
>
> *Well, I might not be remembering things exactly right, I'll admit. I was pretty sure it was a giant mutant sloth with death ray eyes, not a radioactive monkey, and that it all happened way back in the Fifties before either of us was born. However, I do recall when I was six I was sure I'd be senile by thirty, so clearly my faculties are deteriorating right on schedule. We should compare notes so I can maintain what slim grasp I still have on sanity a little while longer. Besides, I'm sure we'd have a lot to talk about.*
>
> *- Natalie*

At the end of the letter, she had included her email address.

Joel had googled Milan, but not Natalie. He soon discovered that a Natalie Donaldson taught computer design at a local community college in Edinburgh. The photograph on the college website looked an awful lot like the one she had sent him.

* * *

'Oh man. Oh Jesus.' Phil held Natalie's picture out at arm's length. 'You've been catfished.'

Joel stared at him, perplexed. 'I've been what?'

'Tricked,' said Phil, tossing the picture back over. 'Conned. Ask her to Skype and I bet she won't because then you'd know she was faking. Why even waste your time, dude?'

'I'll admit to being a little surprised,' said Chase, giving him a stare, 'after hearing how things went the other night with Sherylyn.'

'I don't like being set up,' said Joel, 'and neither did she. Sure, she was nice, but I bet she told Marge she's not interested in taking things any further. It was a one-off.'

'So…something happened?' asked Phil, looking between them. Joel nodded. 'And you're writing to some lunatic instead?' Phil cried out in anguish, clutching at his scalp. 'Why?' he hissed, '*why?*'

'Shut up, Phil.' Chase turned back to him. 'Marge wondered if maybe you freaked Sherylyn out by talking about your, uh, hobby. Did you?'

'Sure.' Phil groaned. 'Before she decided to spend the night,' Joel added, 'so I guess it wasn't such a bad idea.'

Chase nodded in resignation. 'You could still maybe call her,' he said.

'I don't want to.'

'Because this other woman - if it even *is* a woman - wrote this stupid letter?'

'Sure,' said Joel. 'Why not?'

'Because…' Chase shook his head in resignation. 'Fine. Have it your way.' He looked Joel hard in the eyes. 'Are you sure you know what you're doing?'

'Of course not,' said Joel, standing as the recess bell went. 'Does anyone?'

* * *

The next weekend, he spent most of his time emailing back and forth with Natalie. It only took a few exchanges before they dropped any pretence about Scienceville being real, and he was surprised to learn just how much they had in common. Like him, she had suffered a terrible tragedy, losing both her parents and a sister in a car accident when she was nine.

Weeks passed, and then a month, and they emailed each other every night before finally moving to Skype. Natalie was first to broach the subject of meeting up. School was about to finish, she pointed out, and her college's summer term was drawing to an end. He could see how nervous she was, how much she used her jokes to cover her shyness.

'I've never been to Scotland,' he said abruptly.

'Then I guess I'll have to show you around.'

* * *

A week later, on the morning of his flight, a large, stiff-backed envelope arrived, again from Fredrick Milan. Joel stared at it, knowing it must contain a picture of some kind - an illustration, or a photograph, perhaps. His taxi arrived and honked its horn and he thought about taking it with him, but instead dropped it on the table by the door. Mail from genuine lunatics was the last thing he needed, and there was a long flight ahead.

She picked him up at the airport half a day later, and drove him into Edinburgh, pointing at the castle brooding high on its rock, at the winding cobbled streets, at the pipers busking along Princes Street, the skirl of their bagpipes making her wince (*I fucking hate bagpipes*, she told him). They spent that first day walking around and taking in the sights, although she steered him away from the castle, claiming it was a tourist trap. Instead they climbed Arthur's Seat, and he saw the whole town laid out before them as night descended.

At some point she took his hand and led him back to her cramped third-floor flat where they made noisy love until dawn.

* * *

'So why did you write in the first place?' he asked, as the first grey light showed through her bedroom window.

'I saw your picture on the gallery website. You had this look about you like you were lost. Then I read about how you lost your family, and it reminded me of me. '

'You saw my picture online and you were struck by my overwhelming beauty?'

She punched his shoulder playfully. 'I don't know. Why does anyone do anything? I hate sitting around and waiting for things to happen. I'd rather make them happen, wouldn't you?'

'So basically you just felt sorry for me,' he said with a grin.

* * *

They took off in her ageing Volkswagen and went for a long weekend drive through the Highlands. He told her about the show, and how his sister had been the one who first put the gallery in touch with him, and how some other gallery in New York now wanted to put Scienceville on display.

'That's amazing!' she exclaimed. She was wearing the same grey slicker she'd worn in the photograph, taken, he learned, by an ex-boyfriend who went travelling in South America and never came back. 'Why didn't you tell me before?'

'I only got the email the day before I flew over.'

'Then I guess you've got extra motivation to finish the map,' she said, steering carefully past some sheep that had invaded the narrow road ahead.

'What makes you think it isn't finished already?'

'You said it wasn't finished. That there was still more to be done.'

He was pretty sure he hadn't said anything of the kind. 'I only made the map in the first place to keep myself together after Dale died. It's nice having the attention, but…I thought even before I came over here that maybe it was time to stop.' He reached out and squeezed her arm. 'Maybe I don't need it any more.'

'Well, maybe you shouldn't stop,' she said. 'Not if you don't think it's finished.'

He laughed uneasily. 'What does it matter? I'm glad I did it, because it brought me here. Maybe I'll do something else now, something completely different and see if they want to put that in an art gallery too.'

'You shouldn't do that,' she said, her voice abrupt.

He stared at her. 'What are you talking about?'

She shook her head, then guided the car to a stop by the side of the road once they were past the sheep. 'You've been working on it for five years now. I don't want to be the reason you stopped doing something that means that much to you.'

'But Natalie,' he said carefully, 'if you're the reason, you're the best possible reason. Surely…?'

'I just-' her face coloured, like she was angry, then she seemed to catch herself. 'Sorry,' she said, and forced a smile. 'I'll try and explain later.'

But they didn't talk about it. Not that night, when they stayed in a former castle converted into a hotel, nor when they arrived back in Edinburgh the following night. They made love with the window open, the summer breeze cool against their skin, but Joel could sense something had changed and that it had to do with the map. Why, or how, he had no idea; but when he looked down at her, at her hair fanned around her face and those wide, bright eyes looking up at him, he couldn't bring himself to ask just what it was.

He knew only that he did not want this moment to end.

15

* * *

He woke to darkness and knew he'd never get back to sleep. He made his way down the narrow, creaking stairwell to Natalie's living room and pulled his Macbook out of its sleeve.

It wouldn't start up; nothing but an error message on the screen. He put it back, silently cursing, then remembered Natalie's computer in her office. Surely she wouldn't mind if he just checked his email...

She had two big flat-screen monitors and a large stylus pad for drawing. He checked his email and was about to get up when he saw a folder on the desktop called Scienceville.

He clicked on it and found it full of image files. One, called Waverley, opened up to a picture of a high street somewhere in the American Midwest, but rendered with some graphics package.

He zoomed in on a shop and saw its sign was in Russian as well as English. The towers and swooping skyways of central Scienceville were visible in the distance, and rendered in exquisite detail.

It was like seeing them for the first time...indeed, almost like seeing them in real life.

He clicked on more pictures, icy tendrils encircling his heart. He was looking at Scienceville - but always from a distance. Its towers reached up from a far horizon, or above distant rooftops. There were mountains in the distance, but barely sketched in.

He selected more pictures and found himself looking at parts of Scienceville that had never been put in a show, posted online or seen by anyone but him. When he checked the dates, he discovered to his shock that some were apparently more than five years old...

A creak, from behind.

He turned to find Natalie standing by the door in a t-shirt that hung down to her bare knees. To his surprise, she looked as frightened as he felt.

'How long has this been going on?' he asked, the air cool and moist in his lungs.

'It's not what you think it is,' she said, her voice husky.

He gestured at the screen, suddenly all too aware that he would have to get past her if he wanted to get out of the house. 'How could you have known about all this before you even heard from me? How is it even possible?' A thought occurred to him. 'I told you about the letter from Milan. Was that really you?'

'No. Look, I...' She pushed a hand against her temple, sweeping it back through her hair. 'No, but I do know him. We talked about how to approach you, and Fred...well, he kind of jumped the gun, so we-'

'We?' Joel nearly shouted. 'Who the hell is *we*?'

'All right,' she said with a shaky breath. 'Cards on the table. There are maybe a dozen of us, including me and Fredrick Milan. We found each other online. There's this book...'

The book, Joel learned, was called Scienceville. It had been published some in the 1950s by an obscure writer called Wolfgang Ramble, and told the story of a town that changed the history of the world and ushered in an era of unlimited peace and prosperity. Ramble never published anything else, and both he and his book soon faded into obscurity.

Milan, then still a young man, and having already dreamt of that same imagined city long before he first stumbled across the book, immediately wrote to Ramble.

'I saw Milan's art online,' said Joel, remembering the un-opened mail from Milan back home. 'I didn't see anything

17

that made me think of Scienceville.'

'That's because none of that stuff is online,' she explained. 'But I can show you.'

No one, she explained, had ever shown the slightest interest in Milan's paintings of Scienceville, which were far more traditional and representational than the abstract work he was now famous for. She stepped past Joel and tapped at the keyboard, opening a new folder and bringing up yet more images. She showed Joel a series of Milan's paintings that struck him as bucolic, even kitsch, although immediately recognisable to him, if no one else. If you weren't aware of their significance, they appeared utterly forgettable - like something you'd find in a thrift store.

Having made contact, Ramble and Milan kept in touch. After all, if two people who had never previously met could have powerful visions of the same imaginary place, who was to say there might not be a third?

But it wasn't until the arrival of the internet that those few who dreamed of Scienceville finally found each other.

'Every one of us had some tragedy in our lives that seemed to trigger the connection,' Natalie explained. 'Milan saw his entire family murdered by Nazis. Ramble found his parents dead after they killed themselves. Your dad left you, but it took your mother and your fiancé both dying to put you on the path. And...you know about me.'

'Why not just tell me all this at the start?' asked Joel.

'And would you have believed me?' She nodded at one of Milan's paintings on the screen. 'You didn't believe *him*. 'I never even thought of making a map of the city; none of us did. That you did has to mean *something*.'

Some of his earlier alarm began to creep back. 'What do you

mean it has to 'mean something'?'

There was a wild gleam in her eyes he hadn't seen before. 'Scienceville reached out to us, Joel. We didn't invent it - it brought us *to* it, don't you see? It's using us to find a way into the world.'

A sick feeling grew in the pit of Joel's stomach. He stood, pushing past her towards the door.

'Where are you going?' she asked, alarmed.

'Nowhere,' he lied, one hand on the frame as he looked back at her. 'I just need time to think. None of this makes any sense.'

'I didn't mean you to find out like this,' she said. 'I'm sorry, I just didn't think…' she cursed under her breath. 'Look. Just imagine, just for a minute, that Scienceville is real. Can you really tell me it isn't?'

He hesitated at the door. 'You can't say it isn't, can you?' she said, triumph creeping into her voice. 'You can feel it.'

'It's not real, Natalie.'

Even so, she was right about one thing: saying it somehow felt wrong.

'But it could be real!' she insisted. 'Think about all the things that are wrong in the world. You read the news and you wonder just how many more generations we get before the human race dies out. That makes Scienceville all the more important - and why you have to finish the map.'

'And what the hell do you think happens then?'

'I think it'll become real,' she said.

Joel laughed. 'We'll just wake up one morning and Scienceville's just…there?'

She slammed a hand on the wall beside her hard enough to make him jump. 'Just *listen*. One of us is a theoretical physicist. He says there's all these multiple realities stacked one on top of another, each one with a very slightly different history from the next. He thinks the fact we all dream about Scienceville means those universes could merge somehow. If he's right, we could make Scienceville real. Wouldn't you rather live in that world?'

'Look,' he said carefully, 'when I was a kid, dreaming all this up, I had no idea how the real world worked. Scienceville isn't a democracy. It doesn't answer to anyone or anything, and that's just one reason the world's up as big a mess as it is. A bunch of mad scientists with made-up jetpacks and robot servants aren't going to fix one damn thing, real or otherwise.'

'Joel, I-'

'I don't believe in utopias,' he said abruptly. 'They all turn into nightmares the moment someone tries to make them real. If I thought even for a second that anything you told me is true, I'd…I'd burn the damn map.'

Natalie stared at him, mute.

He went upstairs and got dressed and packed the rest of his clothes as fast as he could. She didn't say anything at all until he got down to the front door.

'Please, Joel,' she said at last. 'Don't leave. Not like this.'

'Then at least admit you made all of this up.'

She stared at him in fury. She had been holding something in her hand, and she threw it at him. He put his arm up to shield himself.

'Fuck you, Joel,' she snarled. 'Look, why don't you? Look!'

A mouldering paperback, decades old, lay on the pavement by his foot. It was called Scienceville, and the author's name was Wolfgang Ramble. Some of its pages had come loose when it hit the pavement.

He stared down at it, then picked up his case and made his way down the street and away from Natalie, he hoped, for ever.

* * *

Eighteen long hours and a change of ticket later, Joel arrived back home to find summer had given way to autumn. He picked up Milan's envelope from the table he'd left it on, carrying it down to the basement and staring at the finely detailed streets and districts laid out all across the floor.

For the first time, the sight of it frightened him.

He opened the envelope: it contained a colour photocopy of one of the images Natalie had shown him. He threw it into a metal wastebasket along with an accompanying letter, sight unseen.

He went upstairs and lay back on his own bed, imagining towers and buildings spontaneously erupting from the soil like great glistening teeth, and remembered what he had said about destroying the map. As if Natalie, or Milan, or anyone else had the right to change history, to judge the real world errant and alter it according to their whim...

He closed his eyes. He dreamed he was looking out his kitchen window, but instead of the row of maples fronting his neighbour's houses, he saw Scienceville's broad boulevards, driverless electric cars floating high above buried superconductor strips and dodging pedestrians and bicycles with silent computerised efficiency. Cargo blimps floated far overhead like shoals of fat fish, and when he stepped outside and felt the warm sun on his face, he somehow had the sense that this was more than just a dream.

He woke, sweat clinging to his skin. He checked his watch and saw he'd been asleep for more than twelve hours.

Then he heard a thump from downstairs. When it was followed by a faint squeal, he knew without doubt someone had just opened the basement door.

21

* * *

Back when they got engaged, one of Dale's cousins gave her a gun and made a joke about shooting him if he ever got out of line. They put it in a shoebox hidden beneath a loose plank behind the toilet cistern.

Joel dug it out as quietly as he could and loaded it, then dropped it in the pocket of his bath robe. He had no idea if the damn thing even worked after all these years, but he felt better for having it.

He crept downstairs and saw the back door lock had been jimmied. The basement door was fractionally open, and the lights were on. He heard low voices, then a muffled cough.

He grabbed hold of his keys, then stepped outside with his cellphone and dialled 911. The dispatcher told him to sit tight and wait for a car to arrive. Then he stepped back inside to listen again and heard a softer voice mixed in with the others: Natalie.

* * *

He made his way down the basement steps and found her there with two other men, standing around the edges of the map. One he recognised as Fredrick Milan; he was bent-backed and frail-looking, but his eyes were filled with a fierce energy. The other, whom he didn't recognise, looked a few decades younger than Milan, with olive skin and white hair cut close to the scalp. He stared at Joel, clearly terrified. A number of folders had been opened and their contents carefully laid out across those few parts of the basement floor not already covered by the map.

Instead of anger, Joel felt only a devouring sadness. 'What the hell are you people doing?' he demanded.

'Mr Kincaird,' said the second man, his voice trembling. 'We came here as fast as we could. We were afraid you might make a terrible mistake.'

'Who the hell are you?' Joel demanded.

'His name is Jose Vargas,' said Natalie, speaking up. 'He's the physicist I told you about. Please, Joel. We're here to help you.'

'Help me?' He barked out a laugh. 'Just get the hell out of my house and never come back!'

'The map,' said Milan. 'You told Natalie you intended to burn it. We are here to prevent that.'

His voice radiated surprising authority. The way he looked at Joel made him feel as if he were the intruder, rather than the other way round.

'I said you didn't really mean it,' Natalie blurted. 'I got the first flight I could and they insisted on meeting up with me.'

'What I do with the map,' Joel said evenly, 'is my choice.'

'You must not harm it,' said Vargas, his voice shrill. 'You would be committing a terrible crime!'

Milan put a hand on Vargas's arm. 'Mr Kincaird,' the old man said, 'I understand how strange all this must be, how very unreal. But despite appearances we are all three of us sane, and quite sincere. I know Natalie told you about our shared dreams and experiences. Until now, all we had were unrelated fragments of Scienceville: but your map, we believe, is the final piece necessary to conjure that world into existence. We have known all this - felt it - for much of our lives, as did Wolfgang Ramble.' He pointed at Joel. 'As have you.'

'No.' Joel flexed his fingers, but couldn't help remembering the dream. It had been so vivid, so real. 'I think you've all convinced yourselves,' he said. 'Like some insane cult.' Milan was an old man, and Vargas was shaking like a leaf. Adrenaline made the blood thump in his ears.

'He has a gun,' said Milan, very calmly, his eyes on the bulge in Joel's robe pocket.

Vargas muttered something under his breath in Spanish that might have been a prayer. Joel slid the gun out and held it by his side with the muzzle pointed at the floor.

'Joel, please…'

Milan shook his head sadly. 'He doesn't want to listen, Miss Donaldson. Nothing will convince a man who doesn't want to be convinced, not with all the evidence in the world.'

'You're wrong,' said Joel. 'It's not that I don't want to believe. I do. But if what you're saying is true, what does it matter if there's a map or not? It's just paper and ink. What the hell does it matter if we believe in it or not?'

'Then why the dreams?' asked Milan. 'Why the obsession? Listen to what Jose has to say - the universe and how it works is far stranger than we can imagine.'

Sirens, in the distance. Coming closer.

'What have you done!' demanded Vargas.

'I called the police,' Joel replied.

Natalie stared at him. 'You didn't-'

'I heard intruders in my house,' said Joel. 'Why wouldn't I?'

'We need to get out of here,' said Vargas.

Joel shook his head. 'I locked the basement door. You're staying right here until the cops arrive, all three of you.'

He stepped towards Vargas, who ducked out of his way, and picked up the metal wastebasket, placing it on the edge of his desk.

He turned so he could see all three of them, the gun still in his right hand, and used his left to scoop up some of the pages of the map from the floor. He shovelled them one-handed into the bucket, then slid a desk drawer open and extracted a lighter.

'Joel,' Natalie begged. 'Stop.'

'Even if I believed you,' he said, his voice trembling, 'you don't have the right. No one does.' He flicked the lighter on. 'If I'd never heard from you, I might have gone right on working on the map. But not now. Not any more.'

He applied the flame to the edge of a sheet. It burned quickly, and within seconds bright orange flames rushed upwards. Joel heard a roaring in his ears, an express-train rush of blood that made him giddy.

The sirens drew closer, then faded into the distance once more.

'He's lying,' Vargas shouted. 'He didn't call the police!'

But I did, Joel was about to say, when Natalie rushed him.

She grabbed for the gun, and he turned sideways to block her, his elbow knocking the wastebasket onto the floor. The gun went spinning into a corner, the contents of the wastebasket scattering across the map on the floor and sending up clouds of burning ash and smoke that blinded him.

He twisted away from her, coughing and gagging and his eyes smarting.

'Put it out!' he heard Vargas screech, as if from very far away. 'Put it out!'

Joel's vision cleared enough that he could see Natalie and the two men desperately trying to grab up as much of the map as they could. They didn't appear to realise how quickly the flames were spreading, or that some of the wall hangings had also caught fire.

Soon the basement was filled with choking black smoke. Joel pulled his robe over the lower part of his face and felt along the wall with one hand until he had reached the stairs beneath the basement door. Then he realised with a terrible lurch he had dropped his keys, most likely when Natalie tackled him.

He twisted around, and saw nothing but grey and black billows of ash that blinded him.

It was getting harder to breathe. He stumbled back down the steps, desperate to find the keys before it was too late, and collided with someone. When he felt hands on his face, he knew without a doubt it was Natalie.

He tried to draw breath, but there was nothing left but smoke and ash. He felt it filling his lungs, hot and thick and choking. He clung to Natalie, but before long he felt himself spiralling down into a darkness that had no end.

* * *

With a soft hum, the fire engine lifted into the blue morning skies to join the rest of the morning traffic headed downtown.

'We found four bodies,' said Detective Harper, 'one woman, three men, all in a basement locked from the inside. There's signs of a struggle, but I can't say anything definite until forensics file their report.'

'Perhaps not,' said the seven-foot, silver-skinned android facing him. 'But if you were to make a preliminary conjecture…?'

Harper glanced at the nearby house. It stood on its own, surrounded by a small fenced lawn. Its walls were blackened, although the actual burn damage to the upper floors was minimal. A small white tent had been erected on the lawn to conceal the bodies they'd recovered.

When the android had shown up half an hour before, complete with the authorisation to take over the investigation, Harper had made it a point of honour to kick up as much of a fuss as possible. First he called the Assistant Commissioner, then the Commissioner, then the Assistant Mayor and finally the Mayor himself, demanding to know why a machine belonging to Scienceville's High-Energy Physics Research Lab had been given the right to interfere in a police matter.

In the end, however, he had been forced to concede defeat.

'All right,' Harper replied. 'I think they were terrorists, planning something big in time for Founding Day. One of them got cold feet and tried to destroy their plans, and there was a struggle. The fire spread so fast they probably didn't even have time to react.'

'I was given to understand,' said the android, 'that no bomb-making facilities were found - nothing, in fact, that might suggest terrorists or anything of that nature.'

'Look,' Harper snapped. 'maybe they weren't building bombs down there, but they did have highly-detailed hand-drawn maps of all of Scienceville's major precincts, including all the research facilities. We found half-burned, hand-compiled histories not just of the city, but most of Scienceville's leading civilians! Add the fact we can't identify any of the deceased, let alone who even owns this property, and it's not hard to guess these people were planning something unpleasant.'

'Almost as if,' suggested the android, 'the house and its occupants dropped out of the sky from nowhere.'

Something in the way the android said this unsettled Harper. 'I'm sure we'll get to the bottom of it.'

'But why,' the machine insisted, 'would terrorists not only hand-draw maps, but make them large and detailed enough to cover an entire basement floor? And why hand-compile information about our citizens, rather than acquiring it online? Why not simply purchase maps of the city?'

Harper had no answer to that.

The machine nodded. 'Thank you for your input, Detective, but this investigation is now a classified matter. If you could ask your men to finish up, we can bring in our own teams and-'

'Now wait just one second,' said Harper, his temper eroding. 'I don't care if it's classified or not, I want to know why a *research* lab gets to take over a police investigation!'

The machine glanced over Harper's head at the smouldering ruins, then back. 'Very well then. But I can't promise to make the matter any clearer.'

'Go ahead.'

'Our current conjecture is that this house is proof of an imperfect merging of an abstract number of closely related alternate realities. It may in turn also represent proof of an underlying mechanism behind any number of inexplicable phenomena observed throughout history, ranging from sightings of the Yeti to reports of advanced civilisations hidden in remote valleys, to unidentified flying-'

'That's enough.' Harper could feel a headache coming on.

'You did ask. Is there anything else I can do for you, Sergeant? Or can I bring my men in now?'

'I'm good, thanks,' he said with a sigh, picking up his jetpack and strapping it back on. 'If you need me, I'll be at police headquarters.'

The charred ruins of the house soon dwindled beneath his feet. He caught sight of the bronze statue in Waverley Park, of the giant radioactive ape that briefly terrorised the city back in '58, and used it to orient himself. Farmlands soon came into view, great long rows of tiered hydroponics that stretched all the way to the mountains and the very edge of the force field that surrounded and protected Scienceville from the ravaged, lifeless continent beyond.

Before very long he had joined the rest of the morning traffic en route to downtown - and with any luck, he'd never have to think about that damn house and its mysterious inhabitants ever again.

First published in Interzone magazine No. 261, December 2015.

Senseless

Bill tasted the sweet, sharp scent of violence in the back of his throat just a moment before the fight broke out - although calling it a *fight* was stretching it, given O'Hare was a notoriously sociopathic brute from Hut Thirteen and Ade, the object of his ire, was a skinny little guy on crutches who could hardly stand straight, let alone defend himself.

Bill heard O'Hare's guttural roar as he grabbed hold of Ade and sent the crippled man tumbling to the canteen floor, his crutches clattering down beside him. Bill reacted without thinking. He threw his tin tray to one side and shoved O'Hare in the back as hard as he could with both hands.

O'Hare lost his balance, his cheap prison-issue boots performing a complicated shuffle as he tried to stay upright. He collided with a kitchen trolley, sending dishes scattering across the tiles with a noise like cymbals thrown down a stairwell.

A whistle shrieked, cutting through the yells of the other prisoners. Guards seized hold of Bill, twisting his arms behind his back and dragging him out into the freezing autumn air. They came to a halt and he listened as the guards unlocked a door before shoving him inside.

He sprawled on icy concrete, listening as the guards locked the door again before retreating back across the compound.

* * *

He waited there, shivering and hungry, for three days before another guard brought him a bowl of hot broth that sank down his throat like a tiny burning star. He'd barely had time to taste it before his wrists were cuffed behind his back and he was led back across the prison compound and inside the main building, recognisable by its distinctive echoes. There he waited, the guard's hand never leaving his shoulder, until a buzzer sounded and he was led through a door.

'You're new,' he said, standing at the threshold of the interrogation room.

'How do you know?' The woman's voice had a slight Scottish lilt to it. 'It says in your records that you're blind, Mr Sharpe.'

'I...' Bill realised he'd slipped badly. Hunger and cold would do that to you. 'I just guessed.'

The truth was that Bill knew everyone in the camp by their scent, and hers was unfamiliar, burdened as it was by the unusually rich perfume of the soap she had used that morning.

The guard led Bill forward and pushed him into a chair. He sat clumsily. He could sense, but not see, the desk before him, and the woman sitting behind it. He pictured her as having very white skin, with narrow lips and red hair pulled back in a tight bun above a National Unity uniform.

'My name is Hannegan,' she said. 'I'm with the Office of Investigations. And you're correct - I am new. So why don't we start with you telling me why you attacked Mr O'Hare the other day?'

'*He* attacked Ade - I share a hut with him. Ade has to use crutches. It's a struggle for him to stay upright or even hold onto a tray. I usually help him, but O'Hare pushed between us in line when we got there that morning. I guess he got tired of waiting for Ade to collect his morning ration.'

'Who is this Ade?' she asked, confused.

'Adebayo,' said Bill.

'Ah.' Bill heard the sound of a pencil pressed against paper. 'Adebayo Afolayan. An African. Another Senseless.'

'He's from Leeds, not Africa.'

The guard, still standing behind him, cuffed Bill across the back of the head. 'Don't try and be smart.'

'And that was reason enough for you to attack O'Hare?' Hannegan pressed.

'Ade is on *crutches*,' said Bill. 'How the hell was he going to defend himself? He's disabled!'

'Yes, but no one is disabled unless they choose to be,' the woman pointed out.

'It's not his choice to-' Bill managed to stop himself before the rest of the words slipped out.

Fingers tapped on a desktop. 'But it *is* his choice,' Hannegan continued, with more than a hint of satisfaction. 'The same as it's your choice to be blind. Give us even just one name, and I'll have you taken to the clinic right now and have your eyesight restored.' He heard her chair creak beneath her. 'According to these records, you've held out on us for two years. I'd almost think, Mr Sharpe, that you *like* being blind. You can go now.'

The guard pulled Bill up and out of his seat before leading him back across the room.

'Oh, and if you don't mind me asking,' said Hannegan, just before the guard pulled the door open again, 'how did you know O'Hare attacked your friend, and not someone else?'

Bill didn't turn around. 'I didn't. Someone told me after the fact.'

'Who, Mr Sharpe? You were immediately placed in solitary for several days. There's no one who could have told you.'

Bill shrugged, working to make the gesture look casual. 'I guess someone shouted his name.'

* * *

On the way back out, Bill caught Ade's scent, and guessed he was next to be interviewed.

The guard led him back out past the canteen building, then further uphill to the shale-roofed wooden hut that had been his home on the island for the last hundred weeks. As soon as he was inside and the guard was gone, he felt Owen's fingers pressing against his bare forearm, tracing out letters.

Big problem, wrote Owen. *Someone new coming.*

'I know,' Bill said, turning to where he knew Owen was. They'd made Owen deaf as well as mute, but he'd learned to be an efficient lipreader. 'I just met her. Hannegan. She must be the new interrogator.'

Owen shook Bill's arm violently. *No*, he wrote. *Another Senseless. Tonight.*

The words brought Bill a jolt of alarm. 'In our hut?'

Yes, Owen drew, his scent heavy with fear. *Change plans?*

Bill licked his lips, scenting even his own fear. 'I don't know,' he said. 'Does Ade know about this?'

Yes.

Well, that was something, anyway. Ade could at least speak, even if they'd taken away his sense of proprioception.

'Wait until Ade's back,' said Bill. 'Then we'll talk more.'

Ade returned an hour later, stumbling like a drunkard even with the aid of his crutches. Bill listened to the sound of his carefully measured movements as he made his way across the hut. He'd been a concert pianist before his arrest, but nowadays he'd be lucky to sit on a piano stool without sliding straight off.

'There you are,' said Ade, falling into a chair by the hut's single table. He leaned back, anchoring himself to the back of the chair by hooking his arms over it, his legs sprawled before him at an awkward angle. 'I saw you back there.'

Bill nodded. 'You spoke with that new interrogator?'

Ade nodded. 'She's been talking to all the Senseless prisoners, it seems.'

'What does she look like?' Bill asked suddenly.

'Why don't you tell me?'

'Red hair, pale skin? Hair in a bun?'

Ade laughed with delight. 'How the hell do you always *know*?'

A long time ago - before the plagues, the crop failures, the toxic algal blooms slowly but surely killing the oceans and the concomitant collapse in social order - Bill had read about something called blindsight. In certain circumstances, if their optic nerves weren't damaged, the blind could see - after a fashion. Even though the visual data wasn't reaching the conscious part of their brain, they were nonetheless aware of their surroundings on an unconscious level, precisely as if they remained sighted. Somehow, Bill didn't need to see Hannegan's face to know what she looked like: on some deep-wired level he just *knew*.

Bill shrugged. 'Owen said there's someone coming to stay with us?'

'We got the news while you were locked up.'

'We only have three bunks in here. There's no room!'

'Does it matter?' Ade's scent was heavy with anxiety. 'We're supposed to be escaping from this miserable shithole - how are we going to do that with somebody new in here with us? How do we know we can trust him?'

'I don't know,' Bill replied. The timing couldn't have been

worse. 'Maybe let's just wait and see who we get first.'

* * *

Late that night, Bill woke to the sound of boots crossing the muddy ground outside their hut. The door slammed open and Bill counted three pairs of boots thudding across the uneven floorboards. Two were undoubtedly guards, but the third man's gait was ponderous, stumbling.

The guards left, leaving the stranger alone with them.

Owen wouldn't have heard them enter, but the freezing wind that came through the door was enough to rouse him. Bill heard his feet touch the floorboards.

'Jesus,' Ade swore. 'Reilly fucking *Burns*?'

Bill climbed out of his bunk, his heart beating wildly. 'Are you serious? Reilly, is that you?'

The man gave no answer.

'I think he might be deaf,' said Ade.

Bill found his way over to their new hut-mate and grasped him by the forearm. 'I can't hear anything,' said Reilly, his words thick and slurred.

'Over here,' said Bill, guiding him to the table and helping him sit. Ade's crutches clicked as he came over to join them, half-falling into another chair.

Owen came to stand beside Bill, rapidly pressing letters into his skin. *It's Reilly Burns.*

Bill touched Owen's face and turned towards him. 'I know. He's deaf. Go get your slate - we need to find out what's happened to him.'

Bill tried to steady his thoughts while Owen hurried back to his bunk. A lot of people had looked up to Burns, until he disappeared during the first wave of arrests.

35

Owen returned with the small slate board he used to communicate with people from outside their hut. Bill heard the scrawl of chalk as Owen wrote out a question.

'They caught up with me a couple of weeks ago,' Reilly said. His tone was ponderous and careful, presumably because he couldn't hear his own voice. 'I was in a safe house, in Birmingham, helping to organise a strike. Unity troops stormed the place but I was the only one they caught. I refused to give them any names, so they took my hearing away.'

Owen pressed fingers into Bill's arm. *We can take him with us. We can trust Reilly.*

'Of course,' said Bill. This was Reilly Burns, after all, famous - or infamous, depending on your politics - for his stirring denunciation of National Unity in Parliament, just days before they seized power. If they could trust anyone, thought Bill, they could surely trust him. And yet he felt a powerful sense of disquiet, as if something were terribly wrong, although he could not have said why.

* * *

Burns had his own questions, of course. He learned Bill's blindness was a punishment for articles he'd written denouncing National Unity. Ade had refused to disclose the names of fellow musicians who'd similarly spoken out. Owen, by contrast, was a computer technician who'd never learned the reason for his arrest.

'How long have you all been here on this island?' asked Burns.

'Nearly two years,' said Ade. He spoke for Bill's benefit, chalking the words down for Reilly and Owen to read. 'We're stuck here unless we give them names we don't even have.'

'What about the rest of the inmates?'

Bill shook his head. 'Most are regular prisoners - people caught hoarding or scavenging. There are mines on the Greenland coast that opened up when the ice melted. Most of them wind up there after a couple of months.'

Ade paused in his writing. 'We should tell Reilly,' he said to Bill. 'About our escape plan.'

'I'm not sure.'

'Why not?' Ade insisted. 'Reilly Burns is a goddamn hero! Nobody else had the balls to say the things he did, even when he knew what would happen to him.'

'Let me talk to my contact first,' Bill insisted.

'What are you saying?' slurred Reilly, watching them argue.

'Tell him we're trying to figure out why they brought him here,' said Bill, suddenly realising what had so disquieted him. Reilly's skin smelled of soap - the same one Hannegan used.

Not that that meant anything on its own, of course. But it was perfumed, and utterly unlike the coarse stuff they gave them in the camp.

'Ask him,' said Bill, 'if he spoke with Hannegan.'

Scritch scratch. 'No,' said Reilly, after a short pause.

'Not at all? A woman with red hair and very pale skin?'

'No,' Reilly repeated. 'I don't know that name.'

Reilly Burns was lying. Bill felt it deep in his bones. They'd taken his sight, but he'd gained so much more; the helmet had made him into a human lie detector. The same enhanced senses had warned him when O'Hare was about to lash out at Ade. He could smell the deceit on Reilly's breath, commingled with the perfumed scent of the soap.

Even then, Bill wanted to believe he was wrong. A part of him wondered if perhaps his senses weren't so as accurate as he had come to believe; perhaps there was some other, perfectly reasonable explanation.

If only he could think of one.

* * *

Owen gave Reilly his bunk for the night, taking a thin blanket for himself and curling up on the hard floorboards. Reilly slept like the dead, which made it easier for Bill to slip out before dawn, carefully prying up first one loose floorboard, then another, pausing from time to time when Reilly shifted or muttered in his sleep. He could sense Ade watching him silently in the dark from his own bunk.

Bill climbed down into the narrow space beneath the hut, which stood on pilings. A gorse bush had grown up next to their hut, obscuring a section of the barbed-wire fence that surrounded the camp. Some weeks before, Bill had sneaked down on several successive nights and had dug a shallow pit under the fence where the bush hid it from view. There was just enough of a gap that he could squirm his way under the wire.

He emerged outside the camp and scuttled through wild grass, bent low. His blindsight told him it was a moonless night, and he tasted salt from the Atlantic. The freezing wind blowing across the island, somewhere off the coast of Scotland, was enough to shrivel the skin beneath his shirt.

The remains of a village stood just a few hundred metres from the camp. He made his way to a house just above the high tide-line; much of the village had become submerged over the years as the waters rose.

After its original occupants fled, the village had briefly served as an evacuation point for refugees fleeing the plagues. Many of them had left their luggage behind, and a few months before, a number of the inmates had been set to digging through the half-rotted suitcases, keeping anything useful and heaping the rest in a pile to be burned.

Owen had found a child's toy computer, and risked serious punishment smuggling it back to their hut. It was a cheap little plastic thing, but it could be hand-cranked, and had some limited voice interactivity. To their shock, it worked on the first try. Owen, who had been a sysop before his arrest, even found a way to log undetected into the camp's network and send encrypted messages to the resistance on the mainland.

The computer was wrapped in oilskins, pushed to the back of a shelf in the sodden basement of the house. Keeping the computer anywhere inside the camp perimeter was out of the question: there was too much risk of it being found during a raid. And blind or not, in many ways Bill was the least handicapped of the three of them. He brought it up to the living-room and, crouched on the edge of a half-rotted table, cranked the machine's tiny pink plastic handle until it emitted a tinny bell-like sound.

Owen had set the machine up so that it spoke each letter when he pressed it. He'd had enough practice by now it didn't take too long to compose an email and send it.

Reilly Burns arrived at camp, he wrote. *Took us by surprise. Should we bring him?*

The reply came only minutes later. Sometimes he waited hours.

Bring him to evac point if it's safe. We'll make room. Is he in good health?

They took away his hearing. Can I give him any news? He thought for a moment. *Does he have any family? Anyone on the outside he needs to know about?*

Another long wait followed. He blew on his hands, then tucked them into his armpits. Surprise raids on the huts were not unknown, although there hadn't been one in months. If one was ordered tonight, it would be worth all their lives if they discovered him missing.

The reply finally came. *No such news. His family all died in a Unity camp on the Isle of Man two years ago.* The computer read the words out in a childish falsetto.

Bill shut the computer down, put it back in its oilskins, then sat back on his haunches, thinking. Planning their escape had taken months. Just twenty-four hours from now, they'd slip under the fence and board a trawler that would carry them to Europe.

That same sense of unease refused to leave him, no matter how hard he tried to ignore it. Bill made his way back to camp, taking care not to make a sound as he climbed back through the floorboards. He needn't have worried: Reilly was still sleeping the sleep of the dead.

* * *

Reilly accompanied them to the canteen later that morning. Bill held onto his sleeve, so Reilly could "guide" him there. Bill didn't need the help, of course, but he didn't want Reilly, or anyone else, to know that.

'Is it safe to talk here?' asked Reilly once they were all gathered around a table.

'It's noisy,' Bill said quietly, sipping his broth. 'That helps.' He heard Ade scratching the words onto Owen's slate before showing them to Reilly.

'Is our hut bugged?'

Bill shrugged. 'I don't think anyone cares enough about us

40

out here at the end of the world. Mostly, we get left the hell alone - although I think Hannegan is looking to change all that.'

'Who is she?' asked Reilly, reading Owen's slate.

Bill could taste the man's evasiveness. 'She strikes me as the kind of person,' said Bill, 'who thinks she can get results where others can't.'

'These people...' Reilly made an exasperated sound. 'That thing they call the helmet started out as a medical miracle, you know that?' Bill nodded. 'A way to cure blindness, deafness, a list of ailments and disabilities a mile long.'

'And they turned it into a weapon,' muttered Ade. 'That's Unity for you.'

'You had a family, right?' Bill asked, not caring if the question seemed abrupt. 'What happened to them?'

'I...' Reilly's sudden indecision tasted tart and sharp, like he couldn't figure out the right response. 'They were arrested and put in a camp. They... they died.'

'Jesus,' said Ade. 'I'm sorry.'

'I'm sorry too,' said Bill, fighting not to show his confusion and anger. Reilly was lying - which probably meant his family were still alive, whatever the resistance seemed to think.

Bill had never had a family of his own, and had no idea what he might be capable of in order to keep them safe. Perhaps he should have felt sorry for Reilly Burns. Perhaps.

* * *

Bill and Ade leaned on each other as they walked back to the hut, the others following a few steps behind. 'Don't tell Reilly about the escape,' Bill muttered.

Ade became suddenly tense. 'Why?'

'He said his family are dead. They aren't.'

41

'How do you…?'

'Believe me when I say he's lying. Unity must have kept them alive, and now they're using them to control Reilly. We've all heard stories of them doing the same thing to other people. We have to assume he's a spy.'

'How can you be so damn *sure*?'

'The same way I always am.'

* * *

Later that evening, the first raid in months was carried out while the inmates were all getting their evening rations. When Bill and the others got back to their hut, they found their bunks pushed aside, their mattresses lying outside on the damp gravel.

Bill got down on his hands and knees and pressed his fingers against the floorboards that gave him access to the outside world. There was no sign they had been pulled up, no scent belonging to any of the guards. He closed his eyes in silent relief.

If Reilly had wondered what he was doing, pressing and sniffing at the floorboards, he didn't ask. 'It's Hannegan,' said Bill, standing back up. 'Everything's been different since she arrived.'

If only he could figure out what it was she wanted.

Not long after they'd pushed the bunks back into place and dragged the mattresses back in, two guards came to escort Bill back to the main building. Inside, he scented several other inmates all waiting to be questioned. He was led past all of them and straight into Hannegan's office.

'Mr Sharpe,' she said. 'We searched your hut.'

He sat across from her, trying not to show how worried he was. 'And?'

'We found nothing. But you interest me. The way you move around this camp, I could swear it's like you can see.'

Bill chuckled to hide his nervousness. 'Maybe you missed it, but your helmet made me blind. I can't see a damn thing.'

'And yet we've had one or two reports of Senseless in other camps having their remaining senses extraordinarily heightened following their treatment. You can understand why that might be of great scientific interest.'

'I don't see what it has to do with me.'

'I've interviewed half a dozen inmates who witnessed your assault on O'Hare. It's not the first time you've been seen acting precisely as if you were still sighted. As if you know exactly what's going on around you regardless.'

As she spoke, Bill heard a drawer slide open, slowly, as if Hannegan was working hard to keep it as quiet as possible. He heard her feet move around the desk until she stood to one side of him.

Immediately he knew there was a gun to his head. He could picture its barrel hovering just an inch from his right ear.

'I have something in my hand, Mr Sharpe,' said Hannegan. There was a slight edge of strain in her voice, no doubt, he thought, from holding the heavy weapon level with his skull. 'Can you tell me what it is?'

Bill willed himself not to move, but thinking was far easier than doing. He couldn't ignore the thrill of alarm surging up his spine, or the shortness of his breath.

'I don't know,' he said, his voice tight.

'I don't believe you.'

He knew, just a moment before she did it, that she was going to shoot him. Instinct took over: he jerked away just as she squeezed the trigger, tumbling off his chair and onto the floor.

The breath rattled out of his throat in quick spasms. The gun had made a clicking sound and nothing more. 'You tricked me.'

'You've been tricking the idiots running this camp for a lot longer,' said Hannegan. Her voice was colder now. 'Go back to your hut and stay there until tomorrow morning.'

And then? he nearly asked, but he already knew the answer. Then they'd put him in the one small motorboat the camp authorities kept fuelled by the dockside and send him back to the mainland, to have his brain picked apart.

But he'd be long gone by then - and not a moment too soon.

They let him out on his own, without even a guard to guide him back to his hut. It felt like Hannegan was laughing at him.

* * *

'Jesus,' said Ade when he walked back in, 'what the hell happened? You're shaking like a leaf!'

'I need to talk to you,' said Bill, ignoring Owen and Reilly. 'Alone.'

He led Ade back out into the chill evening air. He could easily imagine Reilly's puzzled stare as they closed the door behind them.

'She's onto me,' said Bill. 'She pulled a gun on me without any warning or sound and I flinched away from it before she pulled the trigger. It wasn't even loaded.'

'Jesus...'

'I have an idea. We've got no choice but to take Reilly with us. If we don't and he realises we're gone, he might alert Hannegan before we can get to that trawler. But we won't tell him what we're doing until the moment we do it. If he tries to betray us or stop us, we'll... do whatever we have to. But if I'm somehow wrong about him, we can still all get away.'

Ade swallowed hard. 'So the plan's otherwise the same?'

Bill nodded. 'A launch will be waiting to take us to the trawler from the beach on the far side of the village, but it's too risky for them to hang around more than a minute or two. If we're not there at the exact scheduled time, they'll leave without us.'

'I just can't believe Reilly would inform on us,' said Ade. 'It goes against everything I know about him.'

'Goddamn it, he lied to us about his family!' Bill hissed. 'I smelled the same damn soap on his skin that Hannegan uses. The son of a bitch has been getting preferential treatment. Do you understand? It's him or us.'

He heard Ade swallow. 'Sure. I understand.'

* * *

Bill didn't sleep that night. From the sound of their breathing, neither did any of the others - all except Reilly, who still had Owen's bed. When the time came, Bill rolled out of his bunk and pushed Owen awake. He grumbled and sat up.

Bill held up five fingers. 'Five minutes,' he mouthed, then did the same for Ade.

'What's going on?' asked Reilly, when Bill pushed him awake.

Bill pressed a hand over Reilly's mouth, then put a finger to his lips.

'What's happening?' Reilly demanded, too loudly. 'What are you doing?'

Bill shook his head, then ignored him, waiting while Owen laced up his boots before doing the same for Ade. Then he helped Bill lever up the two long floorboards.

'You're *escaping*?' asked Reilly.

'I'll go first,' Bill said, tapping his own chest, then pointing to the gap in the floor for Reilly's benefit. 'Then you-' he pointed at Reilly, and then at Owen and Ade '-then the others.'

Bill slid down through the narrow gap before Reilly could say anything more. His knees pressed into damp soil and he squirmed beneath the floorboards towards the gorse bush. A body pushed through the gap behind him, and he heard Reilly cursing and muttering as he flailed around in the dark.

Bill crawled under the gap in the fence. Reilly came next, standing up and staring around. Ade followed, half-dragged by Owen.

Bill took Ade's other arm. He'd known it would be slow going; Owen and Reilly at least could walk, but they'd have to carry Ade most of the way.

'This way,' said Bill, pointing in the direction of the village.

Reilly grabbed Bill's free arm. 'Why didn't you tell me?'

Bill shook him free, then tapped at his arm as if he were wearing a watch and mouthed the words *no time* at him.

'Of course there was time!' Reilly's speech was becoming more slurred; he'd been relying on the memory of what his voice sounded like in order to speak, and that memory was fading. 'You didn't trust me.'

Bill shook his head. There was nothing more he could say.

They reached the village. Bill felt the water lapping around his feet as they navigated a street. He could sense Reilly's amazement at the way he moved as easily as a sighted person.

Then they turned a corner, and then another, and Bill suddenly realised Reilly had slipped away. He heard the man's retreating footsteps as he hurried away from them and back in the direction of the camp.

'Reilly,' said Ade, his voice urgent. 'He's-'

'I know.' The words felt heavy in Bill's mouth. He sniffed the air, cold and sharp in his nostrils. 'Keep going,' he told Ade.

'Make sure you and Owen get to the rendezvous.'

'But what about you?'

'Just get there,' he snapped. 'If he alerts the camp authorities, it won't just be our skins - it'll be everyone on that trawler as well.'

Had he known this moment would come, he wondered? Could things have gone a better way, a way that didn't end in betrayal and death?

He didn't, couldn't, know. There was only this moment, and the next.

He pulled Ade into a tight embrace, then gave Owen a final nod before turning and hurrying back in the direction of the camp. It didn't take long for him to pick up Reilly's scent.

It soon became evident that Reilly had got lost in the dark. Bill could hear his laboured breathing, and followed the sound of his splashing feet down a side-street.

Bill stepped towards him and sensed Reilly's alarm. 'I'm sorry,' said Reilly. 'I got lost. I-'

'You were trying to make your way back to the camp, weren't you?'

Reilly clearly didn't need his hearing to guess what Bill was saying. 'You're not even blind, are you?' Reilly demanded, backing away.

'No, I *was* blind.' Bill moved closer. 'To certain realities, at least. Hannegan wanted you to spy on us, didn't she? That's why she put you in our hut.'

Reilly couldn't hear him. It didn't matter. Without even thinking about it, Bill had bent down and scooped up a rock that felt heavy in his hand.

'You don't understand,' said Reilly, his voice thick. 'My family - they said they would...' He paused and let out a shuddering breath.

'I do understand,' said Bill. He heard the distant rumble of a motorboat engine as it approached the shore. 'And I'm sorry.'

Bill could almost taste the adrenaline spiking in the other mans's bloodstream. Building up his courage.

Reilly came towards him then with a roar, splashing through the water. Bill anticipated him easily in the moonless dark, dodging out of his way. Reilly stumbled and fell hard as Bill kicked him from behind.

'I'm truly sorry,' said Bill, then brought the rock crashing down on Reilly's head, again and again.

A little while later, he made his way to the rendezvous and listened to the sound of a motorboat engine growing faint with distance. He sat down with his back to a wall and stared out towards the ocean, letting the rain wash the blood from his face.

Just before dawn came the wail of a siren, and the sound of voices from the direction of the camp, coming closer.

First published in Shoreline of Infinity No. 4, June 2016.

The Long Fall

Most likely, thought Nadia, there were a lot worse ways to die than falling into a bottomless pit and asphyxiating as the air in your suit ran out. But at that precise moment, with her grip on a steel girder slowly weakening and nothing beneath her but a drop into eternity, almost any other way of meeting her maker seemed preferable.

'So I got to thinking,' Yuichi continued, his voice crackling over the radio as he shoved rubble out of the way, 'about collective nouns. Like, what's the collective term for a bunch of people who're all the last man and woman on Earth?'

She and Chloe had been exploring the facility when the ground suddenly gave way beneath them. Half the facility had collapsed into the pit without warning, along with a sizeable chunk of the bedrock on which it had been built. Chloe got away in time, but Nadia had fallen, landing on top of a girder that until moments before had formed part of the building's foundations.

It was a miracle her pressure suit hadn't been holed. She had managed to hold onto the girder and pull herself all the way up on top of it, lying with her chest pressed down against its upper surface.

'I mean,' Yuichi continued, 'if by definition you're the only one of something, you can't have a collective noun, can you?'

'Just hurry up,' Nadia gasped. He was trying to keep her mind off her predicament, of course, like it was just another working day. She wanted to scream at him that it wasn't helping.

'Hey,' Chloe said over the radio, 'conserve your energy. We're almost there.'

Liar, thought Nadia. Even so, she focused on her breathing, holding the air in her lungs for long seconds before letting it out slowly. The thumping of her heart slowed down a little.

When she looked up, Nadia could see the ceiling of the basement - or what was left of it - several metres above where she dangled. The broken edge of the basement floor was slightly closer, but still out of reach. She'd already tried, but there were no foot or handholds to be had. Nor could she reach the tangle of cables that emerged from a pipe embedded in the concrete floor, and with which she might have been able to climb back up.

A slight vibration rolled through the girder, and her lungs seized up like they were caught in an iron straitjacket. The vibration faded after several moments, however, and Nadia remembered to breathe again.

'Hey Chloe,' she said shakily. 'That thing you said, just before the whole place came apart.'

'What?'

'That maybe someone got here before us.'

'There's no one else here,' said Chloe. 'This whole parallel is extinct, in case you hadn't noticed. Nobody's left alive.'

'Then explain the extra set of footprints,' said Nadia.

'I didn't see anything like that, Nadia,' the other woman said tersely. 'And trust me, we'll have you out of there real soon.'

* * *

'What do you mean a 'bottomless' pit? There's no such thing,' Nadia had said the previous morning.

Kip Mayer clicked a pen-like remote and the projection on the screen in the briefing room changed. Nadia saw a broken landscape on some other Earth, with a vast, perfectly circular hole cut into it. The picture had been taken from a rise in the land just metres from the pit's edge, and just the sight of it made Nadia's guts churn.

'Well,' said Mayer, standing next to the projector, 'the mouth of the pit is twenty kilometres wide, but its bottom has been receding from the surface of the parallel in question at close to light-speed for at least fifteen years, which makes it about…'

'About 142 trillion kilometres deep,' Yuichi answered from beside Nadia. 'And it'll keep growing, forever.'

Something twisted in Nadia's gut. 'I don't get it. The Earth is, what, thirteen thousand kilometres across? So how…?'

'"Pit" isn't the right word,' said Chloe, from Nadia's other side. She, along with Yuichi, would be accompanying Nadia on her first real mission as a Pathfinder. 'It's really a wormhole. It exists outside of the universe, like a three-dimensional hole in a two-dimensional plain.'

'It's really a pocket universe,' said Yuichi, his fold-down chair squeaking beneath him, 'created when the Russians on that there parallel made the mistake of throwing their EM around a particle accelerator to see what happened.'

Mayer nodded. 'Unlucky for them, but maybe lucky for us.'

'EM?' asked Nadia.

'Exotic Matter,' said Yuichi.

Mayer clicked his remote again, and Nadia next saw a photograph of a jagged ruin barely a few dozen metres from the edge of the pit.

51

'This,' said Mayer, 'is what's left of their EM Containment Facility - and that, ladies and gentlemen, is where you'll be going tomorrow morning.'

Nadia stared at Mayer in horror. 'Isn't that…a little close for comfort?'

Yuichi chuckled. 'That's right - you don't have much of a head for heights, do you?'

Nadia swallowed away the sudden dryness in her throat. 'When did you figure that out?'

'When I saw you standing on a ladder trying to change a lightbulb the other day.' He clapped her on the shoulder. 'Don't worry - you're not going into the pit, just right up to its edge.' He grinned. 'Think of this as your trial by fire, Nads. Once we've got what we're after, you can consider yourself a fully-fledged Pathfinder.'

* * *

'How about a cataclysm of Pathfinders?' suggested Nadia, shifting her grip on the girder.

'Nah,' said Yuichi. She could her the strain in his voice as he and Chloe tried to clear rubble from the corridor leading down to the basement. '"Pathfinders"' is just what the Authority call us. It doesn't say what we are.'

'Right. So a cataclysm of, of…'

'A survival,' said Yuichi.

'A survival of…what? Survivors?'

'See?' said Yuichi. 'It isn't easy to find the right words.'

'Hey,' Chloe snapped. 'Stop talking and help me get these damn rocks out of the way. And for God's sake, Nadia, conserve your air.'

Nadia tried to ignore the deep ache spreading across her ribs and along her shoulders. 'How can the pit even have gravity, anyway?' she asked, ignoring Chloe. 'What the hell's pulling my legs down, if the pit's just twisted-up space?'

'My guess,' said Yuichi, 'is that the Earth's gravity field still exerts an effect, but only around the mouth of the pit. That'd still be enough to accelerate any object in a downwards direction, and once it passes out of the influence of the Earth's gravity, there'd be nothing to stop it moving in the same direction forev-'

'*Yuichi.*'

'Okay, fine. Look, just hold tight, Nadia, okay? We've just about got the last of these rocks out of the way.'

'My arms and legs are getting numb.'

'Breathe shallow,' said Yuichi. 'I'll stand you a drink when we get home.'

She laughed weakly. 'That gut-rot you brew? Are you trying to make me let go?'

Chloe laughed, but she sounded like she was on the verge of hysteria.

You like acting tough, Rozalia sometimes said to her, but I wish you'd just admit it when you're scared.

That would be about now, thought Nadia, but Rozalia wasn't there to say it to. She glanced at her suit's oxygen readings: if they didn't get her out in the next twenty minutes, she wouldn't have enough air to make it back to the transfer point. If it came to the worst, she'd hold on to the girder for as long as possible before she finally blacked out.

Because the last thing she wanted to be was conscious when she started a fall that would never end.

* * *

After Kip Mayer's briefing, Nadia, Yuichi and Chloe drove to the island's only town. Most of the buildings were deserted, their former occupants swept away by whatever unspecified disaster had befallen not only them, but all the rest of the inhabitants of this particular parallel. A few houses and offices, however, along with a hotel-bar, had been refurbished for general use.

'This,' said Yuichi, spreading a map out on a table in the island's only bar, 'is a map of Siberia.' He tapped at a point close to the bottom of the map. 'We're headed for this town, seventy-five kilometres south-west of the Tunguska region.'

'Any connection with the famous meteor?' asked Nadia, taking a sip of Yuichi's home-brew and struggling not to grimace.

Yuichi positively beamed. 'Bingo. It wasn't in fact a meteor, it turns out, but just the type of exotic matter we've been looking for. Somehow, the Russians figured out how to recover it. It's stored in a magnetic containment unit inside a purpose-built facility.'

'And something went wrong?'

Yuichi grinned. 'If it went right, it wouldn't be a post-apocalyptic parallel, would it?'

'There must have been a hell of a wind when that hole formed,' Chloe muttered. Several other Pathfinders - all the last man or woman from different parallels - were chatting and drinking at nearby tables.

Yuichi nodded. 'Our remote drones brought back footage that shows everything for about a thousand miles around got sucked up in the vortex.'

'How did this facility survive all that?' asked Nadia.

'Well, it started life as a nuclear bunker,' he explained, 'so the important part is underground. There was a building up top, but that was swept away. Even so, we were lucky to find any of it intact.'

'But what do we actually need this exotic matter for?' asked Nadia.

'It's what makes our transfer stages function,' Chloe explained. 'Without it, we couldn't travel around different parallel universes like we do. But it's a non-renewable resource; eventually we'll use what we have up.'

'Can we really be sure it's there? The EM?'

Chloe nodded. 'A drone got all the way inside the facility and brought back video. The EM's stored inside a portable electromagnetic containment unit that's about the size of a suitcase. All we need to do is walk in, pull the case out of its storage unit and walk out of there.' She smiled. 'What could be simpler?'

* * *

'Sounds dangerous,' said Rozalia, later that night in bed.

'Is there anything these people do that isn't dangerous?' Nadia let her head sink against the other woman's shoulder. 'Last week they had me in the middle of the Atlantic, except it was frozen solid.'

'Yeah?' Rozalia chuckled. 'Day before last they had me in a biohazard suit on a parallel that got itself wiped out by some killer virus. One tear in that suit, and I'd have been frothing at the mouth in seconds.'

'Why do we do this again?'

Rozalia nodded at their bedroom window, beyond which crickets chirped in the night. 'Hell of a lot better than being stuck in that damned underground silo eating paste and breathing recycled air like we used to, isn't it?'

'Definitely,' Nadia agreed. 'When's your first full mission?'

'Day after yours.' She kissed Nadia on top of her head, then paused as she reached for the light-switch. 'They said there'd be actual zombies, and I'm still not sure if they were kidding or not. In the meantime, get some sleep. You've got a long day tomorrow.'

* * *

Nadia adjusted her grip on the girder, and began to wonder if maybe she really had been seeing things. She'd had just that one glimpse of an extra set of footprints in the dust. Perhaps Chloe was right, and she had only imagined it.

'Hey, Chloe? How'd you get away, anyway?'

'I just turned and ran for the corridor,' Chloe replied. 'I could have sworn you were following right behind me. I'm sorry, Nadia. If I'd been paying just a little more attention to what the hell was going on…'

'Don't beat yourself up,' said Nadia. 'I got lucky landing on a girder. You might not have been so lucky.'

'Well, just hang on a little while longer, okay? We're almost there.'

Nadia could tell Chloe was lying. They're not going to get here in time, she realised, her stomach squeezing into a tight knot.

'Okay,' said Yuichi over the radio. 'That's most of the rubble cleared out of the stairwell. Just need to move this-' he grunted '-and a couple more boulders and, uh…'

'What?'

'Nothing,' he said, his voice unusually terse.

Nadia could see the sun moving slowly towards the horizon, beyond the pit's far edge, twenty kilometres away. It shone down on a lifeless and airless Earth: anyone not close enough to get sucked up in the maelstrom as the atmosphere drained away would have had nothing to look forward to but slow, terrible suffocation.

There. Something moved, out of the corner of her eye. Nadia twisted her head around, then looked up to see a helmeted figure looking over the edge of the basement floor and straight down at her.

Dammit, she hadn't been seeing things! She noticed their pressure suit was blue, rather than the dark red of those worn by her and the other Pathfinders.

'Hey!' Nadia shouted. 'There's someone else here!'

The figure ducked back out of sight, precisely as if they had heard her.

The radio hissed for several moments without a reply. Every time either Chloe or Yuichi switched channels so they could talk privately without her overhearing, Nadia could hear a very faint click. She heard it just then, and counted the seconds before another click, which meant they were back online with her.

'How are your oxygen levels?' asked Yuichi. 'Can you tell me the reading?'

'For God's sake, I'm not hallucinating! There's someone in the basement above me, so if it isn't one of you, then...'

Her voice trailed off. Then who was it? A survivor, maybe? Someone who'd managed to stay alive on this parallel, just like her and Rozalia and all the rest of the Pathfinders had on their own worlds?

'I know you think I'm crazy,' Nadia said levelly, 'but we're not alone. They're wearing a blue pressure suit. I was looking straight at them. I'm going to go offline for a minute and cycle through some different frequencies in case there's one I can talk to them on.'

'No.' Chloe sounded urgent. 'Don't do that. We need to be able to talk to you.'

'I'm not going anywhere,' Nadia snapped. 'Just get the hell down here and see for yourself. I'm going offline now.'

'Wai-'

Click.

Nadia ran up and down the radio frequencies, shouting into her microphone and hoping for a response. The helmeted figure reappeared again, watching for a few moments before again ducking back out of sight. Nadia shouted in frustration, but it was no use: they didn't appear again.

* * *

'Okay,' said Yuichi, seconds after they arrived at the target parallel, 'check your heads-up displays and you'll see a map's been uploaded to your circuits.'

The three of them stood inside a circle of field-pillars that constituted their transfer point. An inflatable dome that looked just barely big enough to fit the three of them stood a few metres away.

Nadia studied the map, projected on the curved plastic of her visor. It showed they were three kilometres south-west of the pit's nearest edge. The land sloped down gradually in the direction of the pit, like a flat rubber sheet pinched from beneath and pulled downward to create a concave depression. Closer to the pit, the curvature became increasingly more pronounced; if she squinted, Nadia could just make out the farthest edge of the pit, towards the far horizon.

The ground closest to the pit's mouth was ragged and torn,

as if the Earth's crust had buckled under the strain of the pit's formation. Great mounds of soil and rock had risen up, forming deep, fissure-like valleys filled with the tangled ruins of buildings and vehicles.

'These are the exact same coordinates we transferred to before?' Chloe asked. 'The transfer point hasn't been shifted closer to the pit?'

Yuichi shook his head. 'Nope.'

Chloe nodded gravely, then indicated the dome. 'I want to check some readings before we go any farther.'

* * *

They cycled through the airlock one by one and took off their helmets. Chloe headed immediately for a computer stationed in one corner and tapped at its keyboard for several minutes before speaking again.

She turned to look at them. 'Soon as we arrived, the drones still stationed here automatically updated our maps. Unless there's something screwy with their readings, the pit is actually bigger than the last time any of us paid a visit to this parallel.'

Yuichi frowned. 'How is that possible?'

'How should I know?' she snapped. 'You're the physicist. But look at these readings!' She tapped the screen with a finger. 'The damn thing's growing - it's at least thirty metres wider than it was a month ago. There's a measurable expansion rate, which means it's getting incrementally bigger, day by day. We just haven't been here long enough to notice it until now.'

'Well, shit,' said Yuichi, rubbing at his face. 'Wonder how big it'll get?'

'Just to be clear,' asked Nadia, 'where is it now in relation to the facility?'

'Well,' said Chloe, 'looks to me like there's an excellent chance it's already fallen in that damn hole. But we're still going to have to go and look.'

* * *

Nadia gasped as a fresh tremor rolled through the shattered rock and concrete around her, making the girder tremble beneath her. The stranger hadn't appeared again.

She glanced to the side in time to see a fat chunk of granite and soil suddenly break away and go tumbling into the pit, and knew she couldn't wait any longer. If she didn't find some way back up, she'd go the same way before either Yuichi or Chloe could get to her.

Then she looked up, and realised with a start that the tremor had caused a loop of cable to drop down until it was almost in reach. Despite the trembling ache in her muscles, she hauled herself upright and reached towards the cable, forcing herself not to think about the void beneath her.

Her fingers brushed the cable, and it swayed to one side, then back again, and-

Got it.

But only just.

Nadia held herself still. She was still half-kneeling on top of the girder, a few fingers wrapped around the cable. She gave it an experimental tug and it held - even when she put her full weight on it.

She reached up with her other hand and took a firmer grip. Sweat stung her eyes: she hardly dared breathe. *Don't fuck this up.*

Then: she pushed one boot against the broken concrete and rock before her, leaning back until the cable was taut. It still

held.

The floor of the basement was just above her now. She pulled herself up along the cable, hand-over-hand, getting another rough foothold.

Almost there. She braced both feet against the concrete and used the cable to pull herself close enough to the shattered basement floor to get a rough handhold. She paused, breath ratcheting in her throat, skin damp with sweat.

Most of the basement was gone. The rest of it had fallen into the pit, but the EM containment unit had survived: it was right where Chloe had dropped it.

She saw the stranger in the blue pressure suit, struggling to get the heavy unit upright.

'Hey,' said Nadia, switching her radio back to its regular frequency. 'Still there?'

'Holy shit, she's-' It was Chloe. 'What the hell were you doing, turning off your radio like that?'

'I don't care if you don't believe me, but there's someone else here, and they're after the EM too. I managed to climb most of the way back up. It looks like the EM survived the collapse.'

'Don't move,' said Chloe, her voice urgent. 'Just stay right where you are.'

Who are you? wondered Nadia, reaching up to haul herself the rest of the way inside the basement. *And where the hell did you come from?*

* * *

'So what's the plan?' Nadia had asked, back in the dome.

'Well,' said Chloe, 'I've pulled in some raw footage from some of the drones, and it looks like the pit is actually undercutting the facility. It's grown under the rock on which it's built, which means the whole damn place is literally hanging over the edge of the pit. And if the pit is expanding, it's eventually going to fall in.'

'When?' asked Nadia, feeling beads of sweat form on her skin.

Chloe shrugged. 'Could be any minute. Could be a month from now. Who knows?' She turned her attention to Yuichi. 'I say we abort - we'd be crazy to go anywhere near it. We've no idea how stable that terrain is.'

Yuichi shook his head. 'Except we don't know if we'll ever get a chance like this again.'

'Can't you just find some parallel very similar to this one where the facility isn't about to fall into a bottomless pit?' asked Nadia.

Yuichi shook his head. 'We've already visited a bunch of those, and in every single one the facility turned out to be entirely destroyed. This is the first we found where there's even a chance of recovering EM.'

'It's still too damn risky,' said Chloe, shaking her head.

'So is not trying,' said Yuichi. 'We've been searching for a safe parallel for years now, without a shred of success. We need the EM, in case we run out of our own supply before we find one. And the longer we stand here talking, the more chance we're going to lose it.'

A muscle twitched in Chloe's cheek. 'Fine, then. Let's put it to a vote. I say no.'

Yuichi glared at her. 'Damn you. You know I'll say yes, and that puts the weight of the decision on Nadia. I won't allow it!'

'Hey!' shouted Nadia. 'Stop talking like I'm not here. I can make up my own damn mind. I'm on Yuichi's side - I say we go ahead.'

Yuichi shook his head. 'You don't need to-'

'I made my decision.' She turned to Chloe, ignoring the hammering of her heart and the insistent voice in her head that pleaded with her to shut up. 'I don't see why you shouldn't stay behind if you don't want to go. Nobody's forcing me, believe me.'

Chloe sighed and shook her head. 'No, it's fine. We'll all go, if that's the way the vote goes.'

* * *

Helmets and gloves re-secured, they drove towards the edge of the pit in a little open buggy that looked to Nadia like something left over from the moon missions. She couldn't help clutching at her seat the closer they got to the pit, and the ground became slowly steeper and steeper.

Even so, the pit itself was hardly visible through the tangle of uprooted trees, smashed buildings, boulders and tumbled, ruined vehicles that surrounded it. At one point they drove past what appeared to be the remains of a jetliner, jammed against a stub of wall.

'Okay,' said Chloe, pulling to a halt, 'we'll have to go the rest of the way on foot. Shouldn't take long - the drones mapped out a route for us.'

Nadia disembarked. 'Why not send them, instead of us?'

'Would that we could, but they're just not up to the job,' said Yuichi. 'And this is too valuable a mission to risk a screw-up.'

They walked under the twisted remains of a pylon tower, then up a great bank of earth and rock. Soon, they were within a dozen metres of the pit's edge - as close as Nadia ever wanted to be.

'There,' said Yuichi, pointing. The outline of a building's floor plan could still be made out, right on the very edge of the pit ahead of them.

Nadia's heart beat like thunder, her every breath shallow. The ground on which they were standing was, she knew, in reality hanging over the edge of the slowly widening pit.

She let the others take the lead as they stepped over the remains of walls; coloured tiles showed where laboratories or storage rooms in the original facility would have been.

Chloe led them to a square hole in the ground, with a staircase descending into darkness.

'In and out,' said Yuichi, flicking on a torch. 'We're essentially standing over the pit, but the drones show the spur of rock we're standing on goes down at least sixty or seventy metres. Nadia, you stay up here in case there's any problems. Me and Chloe will-'

'I'd rather go down,' Nadia said firmly. 'Please don't babysit me. There's no point in me being here unless I can do this job just as well as either of you.'

Yuichi shrugged. 'Well…I'm not going to argue, but are you sure about this?'

She nodded, ignoring the clamour of her heart. 'Very.'

'Okay,' said Chloe, 'it's me and you then. Yuichi, maintain radio contact as best you can. Standard drill - anything goes wrong, make sure you get back home in one piece so the others know what happened.' She started to descend the stairway. 'In and out,' she said, looking back up at Nadia. 'Not one second longer than necessary.'

Nadia nodded fervently. 'Damn right.'

* * *

Nadia flicked on her own torch as she followed Chloe down. The shadows were hard black, with clearly defined edges in the

64

vacuum. The ground felt solid beneath her boots, but all she could think about was the bottomless pit just metres beneath her feet.

The stairway brought them to an intersection between several corridors, one of which terminated abruptly where the ground had torn away.

'We're going right,' said Chloe, leading the way. Her torch flashed off signs printed in Cyrillic, their boots stirring up ancient dust. For a moment Nadia imagined she saw the outline of a figure down the far end of another corridor, then chastised herself for being so easily spooked.

They arrived in a wide, low-ceilinged basement, where Chloe shone her torch on a wall covered in dials and screens that, by a miracle, still glowed softly.

'Would you believe it,' said Chloe. 'Reactor's still running. See that handle?' She pointed at something protruding from amidst the machinery. 'That's what we're here for. Long as the container's internal safety systems are intact, we should have no problem hauling it back home. Bring your torch over here, will you?'

Nadia shone her own torch on a keyboard as Chloe tapped at it, using a stylus gripped in her suit's glove. A screen flickered, then text flowed across it.

'So far, so good,' Chloe muttered, tapping again. 'I could swear...' She fell silent.

'What is it?'

Chloe laughed uneasily. 'If I didn't know better, I'd swear someone had already been here.' She tapped again. 'Just a minute.'

Nadia looked around and caught sight of a second doorway. She shone her torch inside and saw it was a storage room of some-

She frowned. Had she seen something move suddenly out of range of her torch?

'Yuichi?' she called out, moving closer to the doorway. 'Where are you just now?'

'Up top,' came the reply, laden with static. 'Everything good?'

Nadia turned back to Chloe. 'Hey, did you-'

She had let her torch point towards the floor. For the first time, she noticed a third set of footprints in the dust.

'Got it,' said Chloe. 'Just need to-'

Light flared around the edges of the screens and dials. The whole room shook, instantly filling with more dust.

The floor slewed beneath Nadia's feet, throwing her onto her back. She yelled in shock, flailing her arms.

'Nadia!' It was Chloe. 'Where are you? I can't see you in this damned-'

Nadia tried to climb back up onto her knees, but the whole room was shaking too violently. The wall next to her crumbled in a great rush of concrete and rock.

All of a sudden, she was falling.

She opened her mouth to scream, then felt something slam hard into her chest, arresting her fall. She grabbed on for dear life, hyperventilating as dirt pattered down on her visor.

When she looked down, she saw nothing beneath her: nothing but darkness.

* * *

It took just a little more effort to haul herself the rest of the way back up and confront the stranger.

'Was it you?' Nadia demanded, not caring if they could hear her or not. 'Did you make that explosion happen?'

The stranger turned and looked at Nadia, their face still invisible inside their helmet. But if they heard her, they chose not to reply.

Neither did they let go of the containment unit. Nadia felt a sudden frisson of alarm: in her weakened condition, she doubted she'd be able to win any fight.

'Nadia!' Chloe shouted, her voice crackly with static. 'The ground…!'

This time, the floor gave way beneath both their feet. Nadia shrieked as rubble pummelled her. She covered her visor as best she could as she fell, but knew with a deep and terrible certainty that this time, there would be no rescue.

She tumbled in her sudden descent, catching a glimpse of the nearest wall of the pit, smoothed and streaked with grey and black. She felt numbed, in some strange place far beyond mere terror, as if part of her was simply unwilling to accept what was happening was really happening.

The mouth of the pit was already beginning to recede, its far edge becoming more curved from her perspective as she dropped. How long, she wondered with a thrill of horror, before it vanished entirely, and she was surrounded by impenetrable darkness?

Then she heard Yuichi and Chloe frantically calling to each other over their radio links: by the sounds of it, they had got away in time.

I'm going to die, she realised.

Then she caught sight of something moving between her and the mouth of the pit - the stranger, in their powder-blue pressure suit, also dropping but somehow moving closer to her.

Nadia flailed, trying to slow her tumbling motion and see better. Again she caught sight of the stranger. Something puffed out from behind them, pushing them closer.

Dear God, thought Nadia. *Their suit's holed*.

The figure came closer, and closer. Tiny puffs of gas emerged from what Nadia could only assume was a rent in their pressure suit.

Then they collided, tumbling together. Through her visor, Nadia saw a woman with dark hair, and slight wrinkles around her eyes.

There was something very, very familiar about that face.

It isn't possible, thought Nadia.

The stranger pressed her visor against Nadia's and shouted something. Nadia could just about make out what she was saying.

'Who the hell are you?' the woman demanded. 'Where the hell did you come from?'

'Who gives a shit!' Nadia screamed back. 'We're dying here - what about that?'

The other woman frowned and shook her head inside her helmet. 'Nobody's dying.'

It was getting darker the further they fell. But even in the fading light, Nadia could see the tattoo on one side of the woman's neck. terminating just beneath her jawline.

Nadia's blood turned cold at the sight of it. She searched the other woman's face, wondering if she, in turn, recognised her.

Nadia glanced at her suit's oxygen readout: barely a minute of air left.

The stranger reached between them, tapping at a panel on the front of her own suit, before suddenly pulling Nadia close in a tight embrace.

Light enveloped them both, growing incandescent within seconds. There was a strangely familiar quality to it, and she realised it was the same light she saw every time she stepped on a transfer stage and travelled from one parallel to another.

Then they were somewhere else, falling through air and rich, golden sunlight.

A moment later they hit water. The stranger somehow kept her grasp on Nadia. Nadia gasped, seeing the sunlight reflected through the waves as they quickly sank, still in a tight embrace. She glimpsed several finned creatures, their bodies long and dark and sinuous, moving between them and the waves.

The light swallowed them both a second time. Then they were falling again, but barely a moment passed before Nadia landed on something, gasping from the sheer force of the impact.

Somehow, she was back on solid ground. She floundered, twisting around and seeing she was next to the transfer point, a few kilometres from the edge of the pit. The inflatable dome standing nearby looked like the sweetest, homeliest thing she'd ever seen.

The stranger rolled onto her back next to Nadia, then staggered upright. Nadia struggled to stand as the other woman hurriedly punched the dome's airlock controls.

I'm hallucinating, thought Nadia: it was the only logical answer. She struggled to breathe, and realised her air was gone. She'd read about people having near-death visions. Most probably, this was one of them. Nothing that was happening to her made any sense unless she was already dead.

Then the stranger came back over and dragged Nadia inside the dome's airlock, cycling them both through.

Nadia felt so very tired. When at last she slumped to the floor of the dome, she closed her eyes, hardly aware that her helmet had been removed, and she was once again breathing clean, fresh air.

* * *

'I swear it's the truth,' Nadia insisted.

It was the next day. Chloe was standing at the bottom of her bed in the infirmary, Yuichi at her side. Several other Pathfinders stood around the room: Rozalia had been there by her side ever since she regained consciousness a few hours before.

Not one of them looked convinced by her story. Through a broad window, sunlight fell across the island Nadia had come to call home.

'Our theory is you never fell,' said Chloe at last. 'You must have crawled to safety before the rest of the facility slid over the edge. It's the only way you could have survived.'

Yuichi nodded. 'Neither of us saw any sign of anyone else. And your air was running out - oxygen deprivation can do screwy things to your brain.'

'Then tell me how I got back to the transfer point,' she snapped, lifting her head from the pillow, and Yuichi put up a hand in apparent surrender. 'How did I do that, with just a couple of minutes of air left? Even if you'd managed to pull me out of there, I'd have been dead by the time you got me back to the transfer point.'

'Is that true?' demanded Rozalia, staring over at Yuichi.

'Of course it's true,' said Nadia. 'I could hear it in both their voices - they knew I was finished. They just didn't want to tell me.'

'And yet, here you are,' said a Pathfinder named Jerry. 'So what's your explanation, Nadia?'

'I think the woman who saved me was a Pathfinder, like us,' Nadia replied. 'It explains why she was after the EM as well.'

Jerry shook his head. 'There's no Pathfinder here that fits

your description of her.'

'I didn't mean one of us,' Nadia replied heatedly. 'If the multiverse really is infinite like you all keep telling me, then logically there have to be other people exploring it just like we are. I met one of them, is all.'

Jerry looked unsettled, but still skeptical. 'That doesn't explain how you could possibly have got out of the pit - assuming you really did fall into it.'

'She had a transfer point built into her suit,' said Nadia. 'She pressed something on the front of it, and boom, we were back at the dome.'

Chloe shook her head. 'No, you said you landed in water first. How does that make any sense?'

'It's obvious, isn't it?' She looked around at their baffled expressions. 'Look - we were both falling, right? If she'd just transferred us back to the dome, we'd have been moving fast enough the impact when we hit the ground would have killed us.'

'Is that possible?' asked another Pathfinder.

'Maybe,' said Yuichi. 'I don't know. Honestly? It hurts my head thinking about it.'

'So she...switched you to some other universe where she knew you'd land in water,' said Chloe, thinking it through, 'as some kind of a braking manoeuvre?'

Nadia nodded frantically. 'Exactly. We still hit the ground hard when we got back, but not hard enough to kill us.'

She looked around them all and realised no matter how much she argued with them, they couldn't fight their inner skeptics - although Yuichi had a faraway, thoughtful look on his face. Nadia let her head fall back against the pillow, exhausted.

'You know what this reminds me of?' said Chloe, into the

silence that followed. 'Stories about soldiers in the First World War being led to safety by someone who turned out to have been killed just hours before.'

'She wasn't a fucking ghost,' Nadia said levelly. 'She was real. More than that - she risked her life to save me. I think she deliberately holed her suit so she could manoeuvre closer to me once we were in free-fall. She wouldn't have done it unless she knew she could transfer to safety at a moment's notice.'

Jerry shook his head. 'What are the chances of something like this happening?'

Yuichi snorted. 'Astronomically low. It's not impossible, just staggeringly unlikely.'

'But in an infinite multiverse,' said Rozalia, 'if it's possible, it's got to happen somewhere. And not just that, if it happens once, it happens an infinite number of times, in which case any regular notions of probability go straight out the window…'

Nadia closed her eyes as they argued around her. She wondered if she had it in her to ever tell any of them who it was she'd seen inside the stranger's helmet.

* * *

They let her out of the island's medical centre later that night, under Rozalia's care. 'They all think I'm crazy,' said Nadia in a dull monotone.

'Not me, sweetie.' Rozalia guided the jeep north along an island road, leaving the town and the transfer compound behind and pulling up where they could look out together over the ocean. 'All I care is that I've got you back, thanks to the mystery lady. And, frankly, it's probably not the strangest thing that's happened around here. Now tell me whatever it is you were holding back from the rest of them.'

'I wasn't...' Nadia looked at the other woman and sighed. 'I hate how you do that.'

'There was something you weren't telling them. So spit it out.'

Nadia stared out at the ocean for a good long while. 'Do you remember,' she said at last, 'how I told you about wanting to get a Black Flag tattoo on my neck when I was twenty, because the boy I was in love with had one? And how I didn't because-'

Rozalia laughed. 'Because the brakes on that shitty little Skoda of yours were so fucked up you knocked me off my Vespa, and I guilted you into at least buying me a coffee to make up for nearly killing me. How could I forget?'

'Rosie...that girl had the same tattoo. I could just make it out. And...she had my face. Different in some ways, maybe a little older, or maybe she'd lived through even more than me.'

Rozalia stared at her, stunned. 'Wow.'

'You believe me?'

Rozalia shook her head. 'I can see why you didn't say anything,' she muttered.

'Swear you'll never tell anyone.'

Rozalia reached out one hand. 'Pinky swear. Not a word.'

They shook on it, and stared out at the ocean, side by side, for a long time.

Guatemala

Bo woke, his throat gritty from cigarettes and whisky, and fanned fingers across his eyes. Someone had yanked the curtains open, letting sunlight stream in through the bedroom window. He could just make out the figure of a woman standing before it with her arms crossed.

'Marcy?' he croaked.

'It's Alyssa, you moron,' she said in a voice colder than an Eskimo's nuts. 'Marcy quit six weeks ago - and starting now, so do I.'

Bo fought the throbbing in his skull and struggled upright. Something rolled off the edge of the mattress and hit the floor with a loud *clink*. The room rolled around him like a luxury liner caught in a heavy storm. Through the window, buttery clouds stretched long and thin across a too-bright sky.

Bo squeezed his eyes shut. When he opened them again, he saw her more clearly: straw-blonde hair and long, tanned limbs wrapped up in a dark business suit.

'Wait a minute,' said Bo. 'Why…?'

'Your friend Shapiro tried to sexually assault me yesterday evening in the bathroom because I wouldn't go out and buy him drugs. That's not what I signed up for when I took a job as your PA, Mr Cooper. Consider this my resignation.'

'Shapiro? Who…?'

Oh. She meant Doughnut - The Stone Tapes' guitarist. Or Rex Shapiro, as he was known only to his mother.

'I've contacted your management office to let them know they'll be dealing with you directly from now on,' Alyssa continued, stepping briskly past the bed and moving towards the door. 'And the record company as well.'

'Hey. No,' Bo grunted. He tried to stand up from the bed. His foot struck a bottle and he lost his balance, crumpling to the floor. 'Ouch.'

'Goodbye, Mr Cooper.' She paused with one hand on the door. 'Oh, and your daughter left a message. As did a Mr Carlos.' She smiled unpleasantly. 'You might want to listen to his messages first.'

Bo listened to the staccato *tap-tap-tap* of her high heels as they receded down the winding staircase. A minute later, he heard the electronic gates out front swing open, followed by the sound of her tinny little Prius whirring through them for the last time.

'Well, shit,' said Bo, staring up at the ceiling.

* * *

Downstairs, someone had removed his new flat-screen TV from its wall mount and laid it across the top of two kitchen stools in the middle of the living-room. A pair of ping-pong bats rested on top of its cracked screen. His foot hit a beer can as he shuffled past it towards the kitchen nook.

'Wait a minute,' he said, looking around. There had been...

A party. Fragments of the night before slowly reshuffled themselves into some kind of order. They'd made their way up and down Malibu's main drag until two in the morning, drinking at this bar, then that bar. At some point, he'd invited everyone to come back to his place, then called Alyssa because-

Because…something. It'd come back to him eventually. Maybe.

He dug around until he found the coffee can where he kept a baggie of coke and laid out a couple of lines, sweeping some more empty beer cans from the counter to make space. His gaze landed on the phone and, remembering what Alyssa had said, he checked his messages:

'Are you there, Cooper? I told you that I wanted paid three weeks ago and you can't even do me the courtesy of calling me the fuck back. You really think you can pull that LA shit on me? Give me a call, Cooper. I won't ask nicely again.'

Carlos, Bo realised with a sinking feeling. He played the next message.

'Called you sixteen hours ago, you son of a bitch. I'm starting to get impatient. Seventeen thousand dollars you owe me, Cooper. Maybe you should-'

He hit the button for the next message.

'You still gonna ignore my calls? How about I come up that fancy house of yours and cut you up a little and see how you like it? I oughta slice your di-'

He hit pause and glanced at the unopened final demands scattered across the counter and the floor beneath it.

Seventeen thousand dollars? It couldn't be that much, could it…?

Shit. Maybe it was.

He called his accountant.

'How much?' said Pat the accountant. 'Jesus, Bo, I've been trying to get you to call me back for, what, six months? Do you have *any idea* how deep a hole you're in?'

'It can't be that bad,' Bo mumbled. 'Besides, now I've got the

76

new studio built, I'll be back at work real soon.'

He heard a grinding noise down the phone. 'That studio cost three quarter of a million dollars to build,' said Pat. 'It was finished more than a year ago. I haven't seen any money coming in, and your royalties aren't going to be enough to keep you afloat much longer. We need to have a serious talk, Mr Cooper, or you're going have to think hard about whether or not you should declare yourself insolvent.'

'Well, I'm working on new material. Things are happening, Pat.'

'For your sake, I really hope so. But next time I leave a message, try and return the call, okay?'

Bo hung up and stared at the far wall. *Got to get to work, kid.* Today would be the day things started happening. Like a phoenix reborn, he thought: the great Bo Cooper, rising once more to the top of the charts.

His gaze drifted towards the gold records mounted in their frames on the wall opposite. In the meantime, he had to deal with Carlos. He wondered how much he could get for them on Ebay - two or three thousand dollars, maybe? He should go online and find out.

He hit up the last message. *'Dad? It's Flo. Mom doesn't know I'm calling. They're having a parent-teachers night and she said not to tell you about it in case you might come. I...'*

Even just hearing the sound of her voice was enough to make him smile.

The doorbell rang and he jumped. What the hell was the point of living in a gated community if just any asshole could walk up to your door without security warning you first?

It might be Alyssa. Then again, it might just be Carlos. He looked around frantically for a weapon and snatched up a bottle opener, then threw it down before pulling drawer after drawer open in hopes of finding a knife.

'Mr Cooper? Are you there?'

The voice was muffled by the door, but it definitely didn't sound like Carlos.

'I don't know who you are, asshole,' he shouted, 'but if you don't leave *right now* I'm calling the police.'

'Larry Espinoza sent me, Mr Cooper. Would you mind letting me in?'

'Larry-' He pulled the door open. On the other side stood a short little guy - he couldn't have been much over five foot two. He was balding on top, with a carefully manicured beard, and dressed in a dark suit and open-necked white shirt.

'Tom Guayota,' said the man, reaching out a hand. His other held a heavy-looking briefcase. 'Mind if I come in?'

'Uh, sure,' said Bo, tugging his bathrobe shut over his boxers.

Guayota appeared unfazed by the TV-cum-ping-pong table, the remaining lines of coke still on the kitchen counter, or anything else: but then, if he worked for Espinoza, he probably saw shit like this all the time.

Guayota dropped his briefcase next to the side of the couch and turned to face Bo. 'I hear things didn't go so well with Dave Radley. That's kind of why I'm here, Mr Cooper.'

'I don't know what you mean,' said Bo. 'He split without any warning two days ago. He said he was going out to get some Cheetos and never came back.'

'That's because he was busy calling the record company and complaining about you. He was here three days and according to him, the two of you managed to write precisely no new material. Now, David Radley has co-written Top Ten hits in two hours, Mr Cooper; he's helped revive the careers of some of the biggest names in show business, and this is the first time he's quit on anyone. What happened?'

'You said he made a complaint?'

'Several. He came here to work on songs, not accompany you to stripper bars every night.'

'Jesus.' Bo sat down on the couch and fumbled a cigarette from a packet on the coffee table to give himself time to think. 'That's where I get some of my best ideas,' he said, lighting the cigarette. 'Did he mention that?'

'All I know is that according to Radley, you pretty much ignored every last thing he said or did. It takes a lot of time and money to hire a man like him to-'

Bo blew out smoke and shook his head. 'Look, I don't know you from shit, but you see those?' He stabbed a finger towards the wall covered with gold and platinum records. 'Those are for songs that came out of *my* head, not anyone else's.'

'And yet you haven't broken the Top Forty since, what? 1993?'

'Yeah, well.' Bo studied the burning tip of his cigarette. 'Blame the record company.'

Guayota gazed at him for a moment, then, with a sigh, dropped into a chair facing him. 'How long before they foreclose on this place?' he asked, waving a hand around.

Bo stared at him hard, then took another draw on his cigarette. 'Fuck you,' he said.

'You've got a month to make an arrangement with the mortgage company, right? Or you're out on your ear.'

Bo's face darkened. 'Who the fuck have you been talking to?' His eyes widened. 'Goddamn that girl, was it Alyssa? Did she-?'

Guayota put his hands up. 'Cards on the table here, Mr Cooper. Either you come up with something the company believes in - or they're finally cutting you loose.'

Bo stood up. 'Stay right there.' He walked past Guayota and pulled the phone down from the wall.

'Who're you calling?'

'Larry Espinoza. You know - the guy who runs Rapid Records? Your boss?' He turned away. 'Hey. Hello? I'd like to speak to Mr Espinoza. It's Cooper. Bo Cooper.' He extended a middle finger towards Guayota, sitting nearby. 'Yeah, hey, Larry? Yeah, I know.' He chuckled. 'I *know*. Listen, I've got some guy here called Guatemala or some shit tells me you sent him and-' He paused. 'Uh huh. No, wait - Larry, I-'

Another pause. 'You can't do that,' said Bo. 'No, seriously, I - or you'll what?' He glanced back over at Guayota, his face ashen. 'Yeah. Sure. Yes, I understand. Look, Radley's a boring asshole. Dude tucks his t-shirt in his jeans like his mother dresses him. No, what I mean is-'

Click.

Bo stared at the phone in his hand for a moment, then replaced it on its wall mount. He stared past Guayota and out the window for several long seconds, then let his gaze drop back down to the little man.

'Fuck you,' Bo said again.

'You already said that.'

'This time,' Bo snarled, 'I meant it.'

Guayota leaned forward, hands clasped before him. 'Twenty-seven years since you had a hit record - a hit *anything*. Five albums since, and I could walk out of here and say your name to the first dozen people I meet and I guarantee the few of them who remember you would be amazed you were still breathing.'

Bo regarded him with narrowed eyes, then pulled the front door open. 'Go. I don't need you.'

'You talked to Mr Espinoza-'

'I don't need him either. I don't work with other songwriters, Mr Guatemala, or whatever the fuck you're called. Not you, not Radley. I could live off my goddamn royalties alone until the year 3000. If they don't want me, I don't want them either.'

Guayota pursed his lips, then nodded before standing again and picking up his briefcase. 'Then I guess that's it.' He walked to the door and turned to look at Bo. 'But wouldn't you rather be back where you used to be?'

'I told you, I don't work with other writers.' Bo pulled the door open a little wider.

'I'm not a songwriter, Mr Cooper.'

'Then what are you?'

'That's...hard to describe.' He patted his briefcase. 'Mind if I show you?'

Bo frowned. 'What's in there?'

'Here.' Guayota stepped back over to the coffee table and opened the briefcase on it. He pulled out a bunch of crazy-looking electronic gadgetry and held it up where Bo could see it.

'This,' said Guayota, 'is what got Zade Valour's career back on track. Same trick worked for...let's see. Mason Bee, Ephraim Eastwick, Carlie Bang...'

Bo stepped over to the coffee table and stared down at the suitcase's contents. 'You worked with Zade Valour?'

'Sure. He wrote *Lines of Departure* right after we worked together.'

'*You* had something to do with that? Lines of Departure was...'

Colossal was what it had been: a monster hit in every international territory outside of North Korea. And yet just before it was released, Valour had been reduced to working smaller and smaller clubs, his audience shrinking as fast as his waistline expanded.

Bo had seen Valour backstage just a few months before his comeback, and when they greeted each other, Valour's hands had been shaking like he had the DT's - although the road manager swore to Bo afterwards that Valour was sober. There had been a greyness to him, an unclean pallor that had made Bo wonder, just for a moment, whether they'd dragged some down-and-out in from the street and dressed him up in Zade Valour's threads.

When he went home that night, Bo never really expected to see Valour alive again. The next time he heard his name was on the evening news a month later: Valour had been in a car crash that left him unharmed, but killed his wife of twenty years.

And then, as if from out of nowhere, came the biggest single hit of Valour's career. Everyone said the tragedy had inspired him.

'So if I go to that phone,' said Bo, pointing at the wall, 'and I call Valour right now, he's going to know your name?'

Guayota shrugged. 'Of course.'

Bo gazed at the machinery inside the briefcase. It looked like the hobby-set of a particularly technical-minded serial killer. 'If I googled your name, what would I find?'

Guayota shook his head. 'Nothing.'

'Why not?'

The man shrugged. 'I work better out of the public eye.'

'Yeah,' said Bo. 'I know a guy called Carlos says the same thing.' He shook his head. 'My gut tells me something's not right here.'

'I can go or I can stay,' said Guayota. 'Either way makes no difference to me personally.'

'Yeah,' said Bo, nodding at the briefcase, 'but what does all this shit do, exactly?'

'It boosts creativity through a combination of cutting-edge neural technology, hypnotism and audio-visual techniques.'

'And that's it?'

'In essence. It doesn't take long - maybe a few hours, plus a couple of repeat sessions. And then you write a hit song.'

Bo stared at him. 'Bullshit.'

'If you've got Valour's number, feel free to call and ask.'

'Did anyone else ever turn you down?'

'Sure,' said Guayota with a shrug. 'Sly Stone?'

'Yeah?' said Bo. 'Haven't seen Sly in years. Where is he these days?'

'Living out of a van behind Grauman's Chinese Theater.'

'Oh. That's…' He frowned. 'So why'd he turn you down?'

'I can't force anyone to take the treatment. But he's living in a van, and Valour is filming a Roast for Comedy Central. Take your pick.'

'I once met a guy at a party who ran meditation classes out of a farmstead near San Francisco. Last time I saw him was on the CBS Evening News, holed up in a compound with fifteen other guys all wearing identical white jumpsuits and holding off the FBI with AK47's. You remind me of him.' Bo stepped back over to the door. 'Look - the one thing that helps me keep my head straight in this business is recognising baloney when I hear it. You ask me, Espinoza's been in LA too long. He wants to renegotiate our contract, whatever. Fine. But I draw the line at this kind of New Age crap.'

'It's really not what you-'

'I don't mean to be rude,' said Bo, stepping over to the door and pulling it open, 'but I really don't care.'

Guayota sucked his lips. 'You're sure?'

'Very.'

* * *

The next morning, Bo rolled on his side and squinted at the figure framed against the light from the bedroom window. 'Alyssa?'

The figure leaned down abruptly towards him. Bo felt something cold and sharp touch the skin of his throat.

'Ain't no one here but me,' hissed Carlos. 'You got my money, you son of a bitch?'

Terror wrapped around Bo's heart like a steel band. 'Carlos,' he said, swallowing. 'I told you, I-'

'No more excuses,' said Carlos, his breath warm and spicy against Bo's cheek. 'Saw that picture downstairs, of you and your little girl. Florence, right? She's a cute little thing.'

'Hey.' Bo's anger momentarily overcame his fear. He shuffled back and out of the way of the blade gripped in Carlos' hand. 'You leave her the hell out of it.'

'I'm just saying, you gotta be careful, man. I got kids too. Want to send them to college, but can't do that without money, right? And the way today's economy is tanking, we all gotta do our best to make ends meet.' Carlos stood back upright from where he had been leaning over Bo, but he didn't put the knife away. 'You haven't been taking me seriously. But I'll tell you what - you've been a good customer in the past, so I'll cut you a little slack one last time - with a warning. You've got one week, maestro. One week, or-' He made a motion as if drawing his blade across his throat. 'You understand?'

'I understand,' said Bo, pushing himself up against the head-board.

'Cause I can come in here any time I like, damn gated

community or not. We got an agreement?'

'Sure.' Bo nodded rapidly. 'One week from now. I'll have the money.'

'I'm serious, Cooper. Don't mess me the fuck around.'

Bo put his hands up. 'I swear. I *swear*. I'll have it.'

'Good.' Carlos nodded like he was satisfied, then bunched the fingers of his free hand and punched Bo hard.

Bo's teeth clicked together loudly, and he scrambled off the bed and into a corner of the bedroom.

Carlos stepped nimbly towards him, holding the point of the blade close to Bo's eye, his other hand grasping Bo's jaw. 'Always keep your promises to me. Understand?'

'Understood,' Bo gasped. 'Really.'

* * *

'Look, can we be quick about this?' said Bo, later that afternoon. 'I only just barely have visiting rights with my daughter, and I can't afford to be late to pick her up.'

'It's fine.' Guayota walked in, carrying his briefcase, and waited until Bo had closed the door before again placing it on the coffee table. 'I did wonder if you might change your mind.'

'Well, yeah,' said Bo. 'I thought about it and what the hell - it's not like I'm paying for this.' He laughed nervously, then frowned. 'Am I?'

Guayota gazed past Bo's shoulder for a moment. 'Think of it as an investment in your new, brighter future.'

Bo blinked a couple of times. 'Hey, you didn't actually answer my question. *Am* I-?'

'This,' said Guayota, opening his briefcase with a flourish, 'is not a simple or straightforward process, Mr Cooper.' He waved a hand across the glittering contents of the case. 'It takes time and skill and dedication.' He lifted out something that looked like a hairnet woven from strands of diamond, laying it across the coffee table with excessive care. 'The science is cutting-edge - originally developed by the government, you understand.'

'And it does what again, exactly?' asked Bo, as Guayota next lifted out a small box, along with something that looked like a pair of sunglasses.

'It adjusts neural patterns laid down by years of habit,' Guayota explained. 'The process forces your brain to make new and unexpected connections.' He placed something that looked an awful lot like a taser down next to the hairnet. 'Think of me as a psychic plumber, unblocking a particularly recalcitrant drain.'

'And then what?'

Guayota shrugged. 'Then you write another *Lines of Departure.*' The little man picked up the thing that looked like a hairnet and advanced towards him. 'Now if you'd like to sit somewhere you feel comfortable, this really shouldn't take long...'

* * *

Bo didn't remember much after Guatemala strapped the sunglasses over his eyes. Although they weren't sunglasses, exactly: he found himself staring at irregular patterns of light that made him feel dizzy, almost as if he wasn't connected to his body any more. He suddenly found he had trouble remembering things - things like his daughter's name, and his address.

Then he slipped into a dream, but one that felt almost entirely real: Guatemala was dressed in a military uniform - fatigues and heavy boots - and with a riding crop gripped in one hand. Bo was kneeling naked in his own bathtub while the shower

86

nozzle sprayed icy cold water down on him.

'*What are you?*' Guatemala screamed at him, cracking the riding crop against his boot. '*What the fuck are you?*'

'*I'm a good little doggie!*' Bo howled, squatting miserably beneath the freezing stream.

'*What are you going to do, little doggie?*' Guatemala screamed, his face red and contorted.

Bo realised he was still wearing the hairnet. '*Whatever you say, sir!*' he yelled back. '*Whatever y-*'

* * *

He woke up with a start as Guatemala removed the sunglasses from his face.

God *damn*, he thought. It had all felt so *real*. But here he was, still sitting on the couch in his boxers and bathrobe right where he had been, with Guatemala fussing as he carefully peeled the hairnet from his scalp.

'All done, Mr Cooper,' said Guayota with a grin. 'I'll see you tomorrow evening at the same time, and the evening after that as well.'

'And that's it?'

The little man waggled his head from side to side. 'Probably.' He made his way to the door and pulled it open. 'Tomorrow evening, Mr Cooper.'

'Sure thing,' said Bo, then went upstairs to take a leak.

On the way, he glanced down and saw his bare feet had left damp prints on the linoleum. *Weird*, he thought, and tried hard to put it out of his mind. He'd have to hurry if he was going to be on time to pick up Flo.

* * *

He made it to pick up Florence with barely three minutes to spare. Bo waved to his ex, Madison, standing by her driveway with a tight-lipped expression and folded arms. One hand lifted a bare half-inch by way of acknowledgement as their fourteen-year old daughter slid into Bo's Maserati.

'Santa Monica pier?' Florence said hopefully as he pulled away from the kerb. 'You remembered?'

Bo grinned as he drove them onto the highway. Over the last year, Florence had developed an interest in surfing. 'Of course I did.' He waited a beat. 'There's just one thing I need to take care of first.'

He caught her look of alarm from out of the side of his eye. '*Dad*. Come on! *Again*?'

He shot a frown at her. 'What do you mean 'again'?'

'It was the same last time! You visited that Carlos guy and I had to sit in the car for *two hours* waiting for you!'

'Oh.' He'd forgotten about that. 'Did you tell your mother?'

'No,' she said. 'Unlike you, I keep my promises.'

'Good girl.' He reached over and patted her shoulder. 'Look, I'm sorry I was a little late. But the thing is, there's this mint condition 1959 Les Paul down at Westwood's I've been meaning to pick up and-'

'But the beach!'

'It's like a ten minute drive from Westwood's to the pier,' he said. 'You'll get there.'

'You had *all week*.'

'I know.' They drove in silence for several minutes. 'This one time. Then everything'll be different. I swear.'

'You said that last time too,' she mumbled, pressing herself up against the passenger-side door like she could squeeze through it molecule by molecule.

* * *

'All I'm asking is a little advance. Seventeen thousand dollars, Larry. I'm taking the fucking treatments, okay? It's the least you can do for me letting that little pervert stick that freaking hairnet on me.'

Larry sighed over the phone. 'Do you even watch the news, Bo? The economy's in the crapper. Most other labels would just let you go without a second thought, you know that, right? What kind of trouble are you in, anyway?'

Bo paced up and down the sidewalk outside Westwood's as he talked, trying his best to ignore Florence glaring at him from inside his car. Traffic was tight, and it had taken a good while longer to get to the guitar shop than he'd expected. Most likely it was jammed all the way to the beach too.

'There wouldn't be a label without me,' he said. 'And I'm not in trouble.'

'Bullshit you aren't. I know you, Bo. You're your own worst enemy. I can smell the desperation coming off you in waves. But you know - you're right. If I'd never met you, there probably wouldn't be a Rapid Records.'

'There you go.'

'Probably, I'd be a billionaire by now, living in a house built from solid diamond. And I'd have a butler, whose sole purpose in life would be to slap me in the face every morning and scream, 'see how far you've come ever since you stopped taking Bo Cooper's calls'?'

'Fuck you if you're not going to give me any-'

Espinoza sighed. 'Of course I'm going to give you the money. You know why?'

'Why?'

'Because if you manage to snort yourself to death, at least I'll get a couple of major reissues out of it. Maybe even get one of the early albums back in the charts for the first time in a couple of decades. And pay attention to Guantanamo - guy knows what he's doing.'

'Who?'

'Goya-' Espinoza sighed over the phone. 'Guam…Toyota…Guayota, yeah, that's it. Can never get his damn name right.'

'Where is he from, Larry? Where'd you dig him up? He said that stuff of his was all ex-government or something.'

'Yeah, well, "Guantanamo" isn't that far off the mark, if you know what I mean.'

'Is this some kind of military psych-ops brainwashing crap he's using on me, Larry? I had the weirdest damn dream when he stuck that thing on my head, and I'm not even sure it was really a dream. What the *fuck* is he doing to me?'

'Forget it,' said Larry, a little too hastily. 'Hey, look, I'll have the money transferred over tonight if you like. You know why? Because I know you'll pull through for us. You're a jerk, but goddamn it if you aren't a brilliant jerk. You're going to be back on top any day now, Bo - can you imagine? Just like the old days!'

'It's good to hear you've got faith in me,' said Bo, only slightly mollified.

'Faith is everything, Bo. Faith is everything. Now finish those treatments - and write me something *killer.*'

* * *

Three days after Tom Guayota carried out his final treatment on Bo, the Fabulous Twins drove up from LA to help him work on some brand-new material.

'Good shit,' Bud T. growled from behind his bass guitar. 'Especially *Devil's Heart*. What happened, Bo? I haven't heard stuff this good from you since we toured back in '94.'

'Got a new perspective,' said Bo. 'You want to try another run-through?'

'Means he got laid,' said Harvey Winedecker from behind the drum kit.

Bud T. laughed, and so did Bo. Back in the old days, the Fabulous Twins had been his rhythm section; now they were two of the hottest session musicians around.

'Rapid sent this guy round with some weird tech voodoo shit that boosts creativity or something,' said Bo. He pointed a finger at both men in turn. 'Not that you heard that from me. It's like my brain's been clogged up all these years and all these ideas just started pouring out.'

'Yeah?' said Harvey. 'What's the guy's name?'

'Tom…Guatemala or something.'

'Guayota?' asked Bud, suddenly looking more sober.

'Yeah, that's it.'

The two men exchanged looks.

'You heard about him?' asked Bo.

'Sure,' said Harvey with a heavy sigh. 'Some things, anyway. Not necessarily good.'

'Like what?' asked Bo. 'I really need to know.'

Bud shrugged. 'Nothing specific, exactly. Just like trouble's always following behind him like a black dog, is all. Just watch your step, man. Just watch your step.'

* * *

'All I can tell you, Bo, is they're just not getting the airplay.'

Three months had passed since they'd last spoken. Bo sat

across from Larry Espinoza, ensconced behind his vast desk like a king surveying a kingdom made of scattered market reports and coffee rings. The LA skyline through the window behind him looked dull and grey.

'What about online sales?' Bo asked in desperation. 'What about Spotify, or all those other streaming whatchamacallits?'

Espinoza winced. 'Please don't swear in my office.'

'I didn't-'

'Look.' Espinoza leaned forward, hands spread. 'We're not finished yet. You're right, Bo - your new songs are great - but not great enough. That's why no one's paying attention. That's why they're not charting, why nobody's downloading them. They don't have that…that edge, you know what I mean?'

'I'm not sure I do,' Bo said guardedly.

Espinoza got up and walked over to the window, gazing out the way he always did when he wanted to act serious. 'I remember when you first signed to us. You were just a kid. Your first songs were huge, but nobody even plays them anymore. Know why?'

'Why?'

'They were catchy, but they lacked substance. Most of the kids buying them were pre-teens, and by now they're all grandmas living in a trailer somewhere. Bo, thirteen-year old girls aren't going to buy your records any more. You need something more…*mature*.'

'More…' Bo shook his head. 'Fuck you.'

'It's hardly surprising, really. Your dad was, what, a stock-broker?' Bo nodded. 'He financed your first demo back in '88. You went to a good school. You never had anything really bad happen in your whole life.'

'What are you driving at?'

'I'm saying you need some grit - and Tom Guayota is just the man for the job.'

'Oh, for...' Bo grasped his head in both hands. 'I'm done with that! The guy creeped me out. I-'

'Listen.' Espinoza put his hands up in a placatory gesture. 'I'll be honest, I wasn't sure we'd hit the mark on the first attempt. Sometimes it's the second try that really makes the difference.'

'What the hell do you *want* from me?' wailed Bo.

'One more try,' said Espinoza. 'Just a couple more treatments, I swear, and that's it.'

'I should just walk out of here.'

Espinoza chuckled. 'Don't be crazy.'

Bo stared at him defiantly. 'I'm serious.'

'So am I,' said Espinoza. 'You'd never walk out that door.'

'Why the hell not?'

'Because you want it too bad. To be back on top.'

Bo stood, his heart hammering with fury. 'Don't even pretend you know what I'm capable of.'

'Then go ahead,' said Espinoza, gesturing to the door. 'Because if you walk out, from here on in it's nothing but MTV's 'Where Are They Now?' feature and getting told by other homeless people that they thought you were dead.'

'I can make it on my own,' said Bo through gritted teeth.

'Doing what? Getting violently assaulted by coke dealers because you can't pay them back?'

'How did you...?'

'He's not just your coke dealer, you know. Word gets around, especially in Malibu. You couldn't wipe your own ass if you tried.'

'You're pushing me, man.'

'And you're full of shit,' Espinoza said angrily. 'Unless you take more treatments from Guayota, the best thing you could do for your career is to climb out my office window and take the fast route to the ground floor.'

* * *

'Just make it quick,' Bo snapped a week later.

'There.' Guayota finished adjusting the net over Bo's scalp. 'This shouldn't take too long.'

'So what the hell's going to happen that didn't happen the last time you put this thing on me?'

Guayota stood before him with the weird-looking sunglasses gripped in both hands. 'What's just as important as my treatments,' said Guatemala, 'is your commitment to your art.'

Bo laughed. 'What in hell is *that* supposed to mean?'

'Do you enjoy your life, Mr Cooper?'

'Of course I - what kind of damn question is that?'

'Could you give it up? Become forgotten?'

'I don't like the way you're speaking to me.'

'Just tell me,' said Guayota, 'what you're prepared to do to really get your career back on track.'

Bo stared at him hard, then looked away. 'Anything,' he said quietly.

'Think very carefully about your answer,' said Guayota. 'Do you really mean 'anything'?'

'What are you driving at?'

Guayota just stared at him.

'Sure. Anything.' Bo thought for a moment. 'Did you talk to Valour like this?'

'Of course I did. And look how well he did, like a phoenix rising out of tragedy.'

'Tragedy?'

'That terrible car accident. But he persevered, and he went on.'

Bo shook his head. 'I don't like the direction this is going.'

'Ask Valour. Go on, phone him like you were going to when we first met. Ask him if he'd take any of it back - if he's got any regrets. He knows success - *real* success - means sacrifices.'

'What kind of sacrifices?'

'The kind of sacrifices that put the soul in art,' said Guayota with relish. 'Van Gogh's ear, Charlie Parker's heroin addiction, Dostoyevsky's years in exile, Kurt's suicidal impulses - all of it helped make great art, at enormous personal cost. If you could make one single sacrifice - something that would wound you to your soul, but make music that lives forever in people's hearts and minds, that changes lives and makes people fall in love or step back from a precipice - if you could, would you make that sacrifice?'

Bo hesitated just a moment. 'Yes,' he said soberly. 'Yes, I would.'

Guayota reached out and put a hand on Bo's wrist. 'Maybe you shouldn't say that too quickly.'

Bo shrugged his hand off. 'Someone once told me,' he said, 'that you're a man with trouble always following behind him.'

'Well,' said Guayota, leaning over Bo as he fitted the sunglasses over his eyes, 'I heard that too.'

'Is it true?'

Guayota smiled enigmatically and lifted the sunglasses towards Bo's face. 'Let's just get the ball rolling, shall we?'

* * *

In the end, it took another two days of treatments before they were finished.

'That's it,' said Guayota, putting his equipment back in its briefcase for the final time. 'We're just about done.'

Bo's scalp itched slightly from the hairnet. 'I don't feel any different.' He walked over to a guitar rack and picked up a Stratocaster that once belonged to Pete Townsend. 'Everything feels the same.'

Guayota smiled enigmatically. 'I have some business to attend to before I can report back to Mr Espinoza.' He snapped his briefcase shut and handed a card to Bo. 'If you're looking for me, I'll still be in town until tomorrow evening.'

Bo stood as Guayota moved to the door. 'Why would I need to look for you?'

Guayota smiled, but wouldn't quite meet his eyes. 'In case there's anything you want to talk about.'

'Wait, I-'

'Goodbye, Mr Cooper.'

* * *

Later that night, Bo slammed his guitar against the wall of his home studio. There was still something missing - the same thing Espinoza had talked about that time in LA. Oh sure, now when he sat down at the piano or picked up the guitar, music came out, and better and richer than ever before. But now he knew just what Espinoza had been driving at: it didn't have any heart.

Sometime late that night, after he'd fallen asleep on the couch with a beer in his hand and a different guitar beside him, the phone rang.

'Bo?' It was Madison. 'Is Florence with you?'

'Huh?' Bo rubbed the tiredness out of his eyes. 'No. Why?'

'I can't find her anywhere.' Something in her tone of voice

brought Bo to full alertness. 'I mean, *anywhere*. She's not answering her phone, and none of her friends have seen her.'

'You called the cops?'

'Of *course* I called the fucking cops!' She sounded like she was on the edge of hysteria. 'She left the house this afternoon saying she was going to meet her friend Josie, but she never turned up. I...' she sobbed.

'It might still be okay,' said Bo. 'It's only been, what, a couple of hours? It's probably some boy or something.'

'Bo, she's *fourteen*. She's barely figured out boys exist.'

I wouldn't be so sure about that, thought Bo: however often he found ways to disappoint his daughter, Florence had always felt more comfortable confiding in him than with her mother. 'I'll try calling her myself.'

* * *

But it was no use. Flo had disappeared as thoroughly as if she had climbed on board a flying saucer and flown up to Mars. The police declared her missing. For the first time in a very long time, Bo saw his name on a news report: *former music star's daughter missing*.

Former music star. That should be on my gravestone, he thought bitterly.

Then he remembered something Guayota had said - about having some business to attend to, right before Flo disappeared off the face of the earth.

A terrible thought occurred to Bo, and he searched frantically through his pockets until he found Guayota's card.

* * *

Guayota anticipated the punch, swerving smoothly to one side.

The momentum carried Bo stumbling forward into Guayota's room at the Hilton.

Powerful hands gripped Bo from behind, wrenching his arms behind his back with such force it felt like they were being pulled from their sockets. He screamed hoarsely as Guayota forced him onto his knees, until at last his face was pressed deep into the rich cream carpet.

'Easy now,' said Guayota, breathing hard. For such a small man, he was incredibly strong.

'What did you do with her, you son of a bitch?' Bo screamed, his voice muffled by the carpet. '*What did you do with her?*'

'Who?'

'Flo,' Bo sobbed. 'My daughter. She's missing!'

'I'm very sorry to hear that.'

'No, you're not,' Bo snarled. 'Valour's wife got killed in that car crash. Mason Bee found his brother dead of suicide. Carlie Bang's son got burned in that fire. I talked to Bud T - he said people get hurt when you come into their lives.'

'They said they'd do whatever it takes to get back on top. And they did.'

'Bullshit!' The room was one of the Hilton's fanciest: there was even a grand piano parked in front of a patio window. 'Are you going to tell me Valour killed his wife *deliberately*?'

'Deliberately? No. But he got asked the same question: what would he do to get back on top?'

'No,' Bo moaned. 'He wouldn't let that happen.'

Guayota relaxed his grip, and Bo managed to sit back up.

'Hurts, doesn't it?' asked Guayota. 'Losing someone close to you always does. Remember Big Fun? Their tour bus took a tumble over a cliff, and only the singer survived. One year later he wrote *Last Train*, and *Rolling Stone* voted it one of the hundred most influential songs of all time. Not bad for a guy whose band hardly anyone remembered by the time they perished.'

Bo stared hard at Guayota. 'That was in the Eighties. You...?'

Guayota shook his head. 'Before my time. But sometimes the creative process needs a little extra *something*, to really kick-start it into gear. And it never fails.'

'You're the devil,' Bo rasped, but Guayota just chuckled. 'I'll expose you. And Espinoza too - don't pretend he doesn't know all about what you're up to!'

Guayota nodded towards the nearest window. 'Wouldn't cost me too much effort to haul you over there and watch you drop. Espinoza'd thank me. 'Has-been rock star throws himself to death after daughter mysteriously vanishes'. It'd make a great headline.'

'Just tell me what you want,' said Bo dully.

'This is about what *you* want,' said Guayota. 'You said you wanted back on top, right?'

'Not like this!'

Guayota hauled Bo back upright. 'You can walk out that door and never come back. If you're lucky, two weeks from now you'll be living out of your car next to Sly Stone. Or maybe they'll find you dead of an overdose in some underground parking garage,' he added, a sinister tone to his voice. 'Or you could sit down over there,' he said, indicating the grand piano, 'and get to work.'

'I want her back,' Bo moaned.

'Tell you what,' said Guayota. 'I'm going to step outside to make a call. I won't lock the door. You stay, or you go. It's up to you.'

He watched Guayota walk out of the room, the door clicking shut behind him. He stared at the piano for a long time, his mind empty. Then he got up and walked out onto the veranda and looked down at the street below the Hilton for what felt like a very long time.

When Guayota came back inside, he saw Bo sitting at the piano, hands shaking as he lifted the lid of the piano.

The Ranch

The room in which I spend my existence is five metres long, four wide. The floor is thickly carpeted, and a television sits in one corner, tuned permanently to a sex channel. At the moment, however, it has been switched off, as per my latest client's request. Opposite the only exit from the room is a bed: a mirror is mounted on the ceiling above, a second on an adjacent wall. The bed is styled after the kind of four-poster favoured by Southern dames in old black and white films set in the days of slavery. A cabinet stands nearby, in which can be found the many implements of my enforced trade, as well as a variety of costumes none of which, mercifully, I have yet been required to use. My clothing is simple: plain black slacks, low-heeled Italian shoes, and a black shirt open at the neck.

There are three cameras in the room - one mounted and visible in the corner above the wall mirror, another concealed within the ceiling light panels, while a third can be found lurking behind the ceiling mirror. Both mirrors are two-way.

The door is locked. There are no windows. This room is my cell, my purgatory.

I pace, feeling weak, dizzy with hunger. I catch sight of myself in the wall mirror: sallow cheeks, a light spattering of stubble, the cast of my face perhaps betraying a distant Italian ancestry.

My name for the past few decades has been Carl Mencken. Before that, I remember little beyond a colourless mishmash of vague images and sensations that no longer have any meaning to me. I know only that that for seven months and nine days I have been a prisoner in this place.

A metallic rattle emerges from a speaker mounted just below the main, visible camera: Josie, clearing her wrinkled throat from somewhere at the other end of the Ranch. I can almost smell the unfiltered cigarette gripped between her polished fingernails, her hair a tight nightmare tangle of tired peroxide curls.

'Mencken, honey?' The voice brittle, old, tired. 'Got your next client on the way.'

I can easily picture the roadhouses where Josie would have spent her formative years working behind a bar, the drive-ins where video store employees and truckers would have struggled to impregnate her in the back of their pick-ups. Now all that is left is a rancid, over-perfumed shell, a dozen carcinomas no doubt fruiting in the choked black soil of her lungs. In the vast boredom of my cell, I have constructed an entire life history for this woman.

'I want you to treat her real good, okay?' the voice continues. 'She's watched you through the mirror coupla times, now she wants to ride the Mencken train.' The voice fractures into a laugh that sounds like a series of seizures. I feel my knuckles whiten at my sides.

'You there, Mencken? Better say something. Wouldn't want to send in the boys with the tasers, now, would I?'

No, I wouldn't want that. Not at all. 'I hear you, Josie,' I reply, gazing in the direction of the microphone.

'Good boy. Comin' through in just a minute or so. No special

102

requests, just wants a good time. Bet you're glad of that.'

I nod tightly, forcing a thin smile on my face. I imagine Josie's life pouring from the raw wound I would make of her throat.

A minute passes. I know what lies beyond the locked door: a corridor, its walls decorated with flocked red wallpaper, leading to other rooms occupied by creatures of whom I know little except that they are like me. At the far end of this corridor is the security room, occupied by beings of an entirely different nature, working in shifts around the clock: men wearing concealing black Kevlar, their faces hidden behind visors and helmets, feet shod with heavy boots that lace up to the knees, powerful and deadly weaponry within easy reach - deadly even to the likes of me. I fear them more than anything, and the things they might do to me if I gave them reason.

Because of this I am obedient.

A knock on the door: small knuckles against wood panelling. I step over, and gently turn the handle, finding the electronic lock has now been deactivated. My client is standing there, small, like me: a little over five and a half feet in height, although some ancient fragment of memory tells me I was once considered tall, even imposing.

Her hair is expensively streaked Texas blonde, and in my imagination her story opens up to me: a life lacking excitement or danger, with only the common rituals of graduation and marriage and perhaps motherhood to alleviate the dullness eating at the heart of her. In her eyes I read the desire for something more, something to satisfy the secret needs that lurk deep within her heart.

To learn of the Ranch's existence, she would have had to become part of certain exclusive circles: perhaps, like so many, a boyfriend or a husband took her to a wife-swapping party or a club catering to certain erotic tastes. As time passed, and her little perversions and games took on a particular flavour, the Ranch might be mentioned: a word here, a word there. She would have expressed curiosity, and would have laughed in disbelief when the truth was finally revealed to her. Eventually, given time, she would have believed, or at least dared to hope.

And now she stands before me, several thousand dollars out of pocket. At least I don't come cheap.

'My name is Carl,' I tell her, pulling the door wider. I smile gently, ever conscious of the watching cameras and the guards in the security room. 'Would you like to come in?'

I watch doubt flit over her features; she's thinking of turning back. Blonde, but not so pretty. Lovers would not have been a given in her formative years. She has, no doubt, developed a rich fantasy life to compensate.

Then she steps into the room and smiles nervously. She eyes the bed behind me. In one delicate hand I see that she grips a tiny, useless crucifix with which, Josie will have informed her, she will be able to control me. This is nonsense, of course, but to suggest anything else would bring days of torture upon me, followed by much worse weeks or even months without sustenance. I had once before made this mistake, when I had first been brought to the Ranch. Never again.

'Would you like something to drink?' I ask, waving one hand towards the tiny mobile bar that sits in one corner. Sometimes alcohol helps them, if they aren't already drunk or high. 'Don't worry if you're apprehensive, most are. You'll be fine.'

Doubt and desire war across her face: I can see the lust is winning. 'You're not real,' she tells me.

'I am entirely real,' I assure her. 'I can show you,' I add, lowering my voice.

'You'd better.' I can hear her heart hammering in her chest: her breathing is sharp and shallow. I know what to do. I take both her hands and gently draw her closer to me. I smile and draw a hand through her hair; she gasps in response. I am filled only with loathing.

I study her clothes. She wears expensive black jeans, and her demeanour and way of speaking would make it clear to all who encountered her that she comes from money. She would have to, to afford the Ranch's prices. I could tell you in that instant of the books that occupy her bookshelves, of the movies she watches late at night, dreaming of her vampire lover. I could tell you how little she truly lives in the here and now.

Her tension doesn't fade, but she's no longer as frightened: instead, she's allowing herself to believe. She glances towards the main camera, the only one they would have told her about. She's enjoying the frisson of danger gained from being alone, in a locked room, with a killer.

'Show me,' she says.

I lean down and kiss her. The harsh light of the ceiling panels leaches the colour from her skin. I gaze past her, at my own, entirely visible reflection, with pale blank eyes. Remembering.

* * *

I do not know how I came to be, or where I am from. Sometimes I dream of places that might be Rome, or might be Paris, or Berlin, or London: that might be a few years or half a millennia in the past. I have no way of telling, for I never kept records. To do so would have been to provide a surfeit of willing executioners the means to find me. Unfortunately, my memories fade quickly.

There is no romance or pleasure in my life: I am driven only to survive. I can last for weeks, even months, without sustenance, but for all that time I carry a raging hunger worse than any of my victims could possibly imagine, because they at least can look forward to the peace of death. Perhaps I also have that option, but having always survived, I cannot know.

Here in the Ranch, they bring dead down-and-outs washed up in canals or business rivals with bullet holes neatly drilled in their foreheads for us to feed upon. It is never enough.

Before the Ranch, I believe I came across those like me only twice. This I do remember: I killed them both, immediately. Their bodies rotted like any other.

My last memory before the Ranch is of San Francisco. I had arrived there by Greyhound. My first – and last - victim there had been a sailor, living in a houseboat in San Francisco Bay. I had answered his lonely hearts advert. We had enjoyed a few drinks in a bar near the sea, while I sat consumed with terrible agonising hunger. We retired to his home and I tore his neck open with a knife taken from the galley. I wept and moaned and shuddered with orgasms of pleasure as his blood gushed against my tongue.

That was when they caught me, as I lay supine in the night, the cabin walls around me drenched with scarlet. I heard their boots approaching across the pontoon, and knew I was done. I expected to die. Instead, they sprayed a gas in my face that made my skin boil and lesion.

When they brought me to the Ranch a few days later, I learned my first lessons quickly. Tasers, whips, sprays and rubber bullets made sure of that.

* * *

'Show me,' she repeats. I stare at her, waiting for her to elaborate.

106

'Your ...' she points hesitantly at my face.

I smile obligingly, trying not to look too menacing. I open my lips slightly, and felt the emerging canines press against my upper lips as they push down. She shudders and pales at the sight, and for a moment I think she might run. I don't care one way or the other: I have performed as required, and the money is not refundable. But she holds her ground.

Now the important part. I again lower my head towards her, watching her lips open in unconscious response. She stiffens again, and I stop for a moment, before continuing. She's been briefed on the rules, which had been long ago drilled into me. She can stop me at any time: it only requires a word.

She remains silent. I touch my lips, very gently, to her neck. She jerks away at first, and then holds her place. She whimpers with fright and desire. I lick her neck, very softly, just allowing the tip of one sharpened canine to barely contact the taut pink flesh. Her tiny fingers grip my upper arms, still holding onto the ridiculous crucifix.

And then I pull back, aware as always of the cameras, the guards.

'There's no hurry,' I tell her, conscious that every word is part of the game. I gaze into her eyes, ignoring the dull pain that has been building in my bones and my flesh for days now, soon to become a soul-crushing festival of agony. I think of Josie, and of how she would laugh if she could see into my thoughts.

'My name's Susie,' she tells me, as I draw her slowly over towards the bed.

'Susie,' I repeat, as if savouring the name.

'You know what I want, right?' Her voice is lowered, hesitant. I nod. The instructions, run off on a desktop printer, had been slipped under the door a half hour before Susie's arrival. I step backwards towards the bed, drawing her along with my hands, maintaining the illusion that I am the one in charge.

* * *

I feel her fingers draw sharply across my chest as I lie back. How many times had she stood on the other side of the two-way mirror with the wealthy select audiences who pay so much for their seats, letting her fantasy grow of when her own time in this room would come?

My arms are outstretched, as if about to embrace her. She is, in fact, safe from my all-vanquishing hunger: I could no sooner allow myself to cause her harm than she could imagine the sordid reality of my existence. I am her whore, her fuck-puppet. I am less than nothing.

I remove my shirt at the prearranged time, as specified in the instructions detailing the intricate course of Suzie's fantasy. I have already unbuttoned my trousers, and they have been pushed down to my hips. I lie, exposed, upon the bed. She kneels half-naked upon my prostrate form and grasps my cock with clumsy hands, her breath ragged.

I become hard, not out of desire, but out of fear of what might happen to me if I do not respond as expected.

* * *

Sunlight does not greatly affect us. Pale skin is more a symptom of lurking in hiding places far from the light of the sun. We are visible in mirrors. Garlic, for some reason unknown to me, burns us greatly. Stakes kill us, but so do bullets and knives, though we can survive far greater physical trauma than the likes of Suzie or Josie.

Once, they set an example.

A few short months before, I had been manacled, chained and marched under guard into an atrium deep within the sprawling vastness of the Ranch. The atrium was open to the skies, and for the first time in many long weeks I saw real sunlight and tasted fresh air.

There were a dozen others already there, similarly chained and manacled and under guard, whom I instantly knew to be the same as myself. I ignored them, knowing I could not kill them at that time. I saw a man – his body wasted beyond belief – chained to a tall steel pole driven into a block of concrete in the centre of the atrium. I knew immediately he was also of my own kind. Certainly, no ordinary human could have remained alive with his body in so desiccated a state.

Wil was the owner of the Ranch, a tall, rangy Texan who always carried a hunting knife on his hip. I had heard whispered stories from a few of my clients that he owned and ran most of the whorehouses in this part of the country as well as operating websites and organising paid parties for the rich and sexually jaded. He also carried a bullwhip on this particular day, and strutted around, eyeing us one by one.

'I want you to know what happens when you try to hurt one of my clients,' Wil bellowed, his voice strident and self-assured, his potbelly pushing at his shirt buttons. 'I want you to know I can be *real* fucking mean when my orders don't get obeyed. I want you to see what happens.'

I learned later that the individual chained to the steel post had been starved for the better part of six months following some unspecified transgression. I imagine he tried to attack a client while in the despair of hunger.

What happened next was appalling beyond measure, and I cannot deny I learned my lesson well.

They sprayed him with hoses, twice: the first time with a mixture of garlic, water and sand at high pressure, which simultaneously burned his skin with the effect of the garlic and near flayed him alive with the sand. He was, quite literally, scoured half to death.

But it didn't end there. Next, they sprayed him with corrosive acids. I watched his skeleton melt: and towards the end, even then, I knew there was something still alive in that melting ruin. What was left, they shovelled into a hole in the ground and covered over.

Always I dreamed of freedom: yet I could not countenance the thought of what happened in that courtyard happening to me.

And so I obey every client's whim to the letter.

* * *

I lie back and let her take me. She manoeuvres me between her legs, while I try to appear as if I am enjoying myself. She leans down and whispers to me, 'Don't worry, nobody's watching.'

I glance towards the two-way mirror, an involuntary motion. I open my mouth, then close it again before I can tell her what an idiotic proposition this is.

'It's okay, sweetie,' she says, cupping my jaw with one hand and turning my head back towards her. 'I paid extra so we'd be left alone. Ain't nobody on the other side of that glass. Now, I want you to kiss me.'

Not so shy, after all. My lips part, and she leans down. I know what she wants: I push my lips back until my extended canines are fully visible.

She leans down, her hips beginning to move rhythmically now I'm inside her. I feel sure she'll come quite soon. Perhaps I once took pleasure from this act, but instead of pleasure I only ever feel a kind of dull tingle between my thighs.

One thing I have learned in my time here. Male vampires, myself included, all have unusually small genitals. Perhaps there is a reason for this. If we evolved from some common human ancestor, perhaps we have some other means of reproduction and the penis has become an evolutionary dead-end for our kind. Or perhaps we truly rise from the grave, but our lack of sexual interest causes the organ to wither over time. For all I know, we reproduce by splitting down the middle every thousand years. I have no way of knowing or remembering, and care less.

Her lips touch my cheek, and I can hear the frantic rush of her every breath. 'I want you to bite me,' she says.

I feel my penis begin to shrivel rapidly.

'Bite me,' she repeats, laying soft kisses across my chin and other cheek. This was not in the instructions.

'It's against the rules,' I croak. 'They would …'

I can taste her life, she's so close: she's a bag of blood, and the hunger is a whirling maelstrom in my guts.

She twists suddenly to one side. She slaps me, hard, and then again. Did the little bitch actually *want* me to kill her?

'I can do worse to you,' she hisses, her irises wide and black. I wonder what she's sniffed or swallowed for courage in a washroom before walking down the corridor to me. She shows me a small perfume bottle, carefully palmed so it is visible neither to the main camera nor to the one-way mirror on the wall. I can only speculate as to how she smuggled it into my cell, since all are searched before coming to me.

She slides the bottle between our bodies, moving it down towards my crotch. I feel a sudden cool moist pressure against the inside of my thigh: the pain comes a moment later and my back arches violently in response. I try to scream, but she's clamped her other hand firmly over my mouth. I feel the crucifix press hard against my gums and cheek.

Garlic spray. My eyes fill with tears, and a keening sound escapes between her fingers. I'm lost in animal panic. What does she intend?

'Bite me,' she repeats again, her voice harsh. 'Make me into one of you.'

No, I want to scream. Turn her into something like me? Impossible. I don't even know what makes *me* like me. My panicked eyes dart again towards the watching camera: but now I'm seeking aid rather than the opportunity of escape.

'Listen to me,' I mumble through her fingers. She's stronger than she looks.

'One wrong word, and I'll spray you again,' she loudly whispers, madness in her eyes. I can picture my skin bubbling under the effect of the spray, and hold back the desire to release the agony in a shriek. Whatever happens to Suzie, it won't be half as bad as what will happen to me. She releases her hold slightly.

It's hard to speak through the pain, but my existence depends on it. 'I can't make you like me,' I tell her, forcing the words out.

She presses the bulb of the spray against my crotch once more and I convulse. 'You're a vampire! You can turn me. You're lying! Make me like you!'

'You would die,' I beg. 'And then they would kill me.'

'I don't believe you. Do it.'

I shake my head. 'I have never made anyone a vampire. I don't know if they can be made.'

She reaches down and grabs me by the hair. 'I am telling you to turn me,' she hisses in a half-shriek; I can hear the growing desperation in her voice.

She slaps me several times again. The blows sting. And then I laugh. It's so ridiculous: after so long, trapped in a room like some pathetic Hollywood wet dream of a vampire's boudoir, with some idiot Texas housewife so addled by her deranged fantasies she thinks I can turn her into something she could only ever dream of in her worst nightmares.

She becomes furious at my laughter, but I can't stop. She slaps me again, but I only laugh harder.

'They're going to kill you, you stupid bastard!' she screams at me. 'So you might as well do it anyway!' She sobs then, muttered curses spilling out of her mouth. The desire for death and oblivion is written in her eyes. She throws herself over me, the smooth curve of her neck next to my face, and begs me yet again.

'What do you mean, they're going to kill me?' I ask, my own blood thundering in my ears.

'That's what I heard. There's too many people heard about this place, so they're gonna shut it down real soon. Won't want you round in case anyone figures out what's going on here.' Her expression becomes vicious, and I see her plan unravelling: she came here intending to force me to 'turn' her into a vampire so she can no doubt lurk on moonlit rooftops, perhaps wearing the impractical black velvet dresses I can easily picture hanging in her wardrobe.

'You're lying,' I stutter.

She shakes her head rapidly. 'So turn me now, and we can escape together.'

By now I'm completely incredulous. But for some reason, I believe her: I've learned to read people over all those long,

long years, to know when they are or aren't lying. And she's telling the truth, as far as she knows it. The Ranch will close: and I will die. Suddenly any other possibility seems absurd. How long, after all, could an entity like the Ranch continue to exist, before rumour and hearsay spread too far? Before it came under investigation? And when the time came, could any of its unwilling whores truly expect to survive?

'I'll do it,' I tell her. Terror and the desire to believe again war with each other across her face. I lift myself carefully, trying to gauge how many seconds I have left. Is Josie listening in to our conversation? Of course she is, sitting there no doubt in some little cupboard surrounded by screens and microphones and speakers. How many seconds do I have before the guards come and drag this idiotic child away, and punish me? Very few.

Necessity can make anyone a great actor. I look up at her, putting on the brave, noble face so many of them seem to like, and beckon to her.

She's trembling. I still her, and bring my incisors close to her neck. Perhaps, if I do nothing, they will let me live regardless. Perhaps I am wrong, and she is indeed lying about the future of the Ranch. But if she's telling the truth, I can defy their authority with Suzie's death.

I touch incisors to flesh, and pause, indecisive.

In the distance, I hear shouts, and boots slamming against soft carpet, coming closer.

First published in Thirty Years of Rain: an Anthology of Scottish Speculative Fiction, 2016

About Gary Gibson

Gary Gibson is one of the UK's leading authors of hard science fiction with a career stretching over fifteen years and ten books, including STEALING LIGHT, FINAL DAYS and most recently EXTINCTION GAME, which received the coveted "starred review" from Publisher's Weekly. His work has been translated and published around the world, including Russia, Brazil, Germany, France and others.

He also has a forthcoming novella, GHOST FREQUENCIES, to be published by Newcon Press, and is working on a third book in the series begun by Extinction Game and Survival Game. A long-time resident of Glasgow, Scotland, he relocated a few years ago to Taipei in the Far East and splits his time between editing and working on his own material.

For updates and notifications of new releases, either visit his website at www.garygibson.net or subscribe to his newsletter: http://eepurl.com/b1ma4L.

30434026R00072

Printed in Great Britain
by Amazon